KT-233-351

Emily was the last person Chase had ex~~~~ ~~~~ in or~~~~ ~~~~ ~~~~opper ~~~~

When she spoke the tone of her voice, its soft, dewy vibrations, cut him to the core— as if only yesterday she'd meant something to him. He hadn't been expecting her and he hadn't prepared himself to see her there. Surely *someone* could have told him she was coming. He could have prepared, could have hardened his heart and his emotions against their first meeting, put up boundaries—not been broadsided, unprepared. He'd never imagined she'd come back here, where it had all begun for them.

That was probably the biggest shock. She'd come back to where he was when there were other hospitals in the area. So why here? And why *now*? That was a puzzle he intended to solve and then get on with his life.

There was an answer for everything, and he was going to find this one.

B000 000 016 2922

ABERDEEN LIBRARIES

Dear Reader,

Thank you for picking up my new book! It is set in one of my favourite towns—Williamsburg, Virginia, USA—where history and fantastic foods are just steps away, no matter where you are in town.

This story is important to me as I'm a sucker for a tortured hero and I adore the strong women who love them.

We never know what we are capable of until we are put in a position to rise to challenges we never expected in life. These two are stronger together than either of them are alone.

I hope you enjoy the emotional journey these two characters take as they find love in each other's arms again.

Please visit me at mollyevansromance.wordpress.com

Regards

Molly Evans

SAFE IN THE SURGEON'S ARMS

BY
MOLLY EVANS

All rights reserved including the right of reproduction in whole
or in part in any form. This edition is published by arrangement with
Harlequin Books S.A.

This is a work of fiction. Names, characters, places, locations and
incidents are purely fictional and bear no relationship to any real
life individuals, living or dead, or to any actual places, business
establishments, locations, events or incidents. Any resemblance is
entirely coincidental.

This book is sold subject to the condition that it shall not, by way of
trade or otherwise, be lent, resold, hired out or otherwise circulated
without the prior consent of the publisher in any form of binding or
cover other than that in which it is published and without a similar
condition including this condition being imposed on the subsequent
purchaser.

® and TM are trademarks owned and used by the trademark owner
and/or its licensee. Trademarks marked with ® are registered with the
United Kingdom Patent Office and/or the Office for Harmonisation in
the Internal Market and in other countries.

Published in Great Britain 2015
by Mills & Boon, an imprint of Harlequin (UK) Limited,
Eton House, 18-24 Paradise Road, Richmond, Surrey, TW9 1SR

© 2015 Brenda Schetnan

ISBN: 978-0-263-24738-1

Harlequin (UK) Limited's policy is to use papers that are natural,
renewable and recyclable products and made from wood grown in
sustainable forests. The logging and manufacturing processes conform
to the legal environmental regulations of the country of origin.

Printed and bound in Spain
by CPI, Barcelona

Molly Evans has taken her experiences as a travel nurse across the USA and turned them into wondrous settings for her books. Now, living at six thousand feet in New Mexico is home. When she's not writing, or attending her son's hockey games, she's learning to knit socks or settling in front of the kiva fireplace with a glass of wine and a good book.

Visit Molly at mollyevansromance.wordpress.com for more info.

**Visit the author profile page
at millsandboon.co.uk for more titles**

This book is dedicated to my friend,
fellow Hurricane Hugo survivor
and Williamsburg, VA, explorer: Jesse Bustos Nelson.
You've been there with friendship and support
since the beginning. Thanks, my friend!

CHAPTER ONE

EMERGENCY NURSE Emily Hoover pointed the way to the trauma room as an air-ambulance crew surged through the department. She'd heard the radio announcing the arrival of the rescue chopper as it had landed on the roof and had even smelled the diesel exhaust through the HIPPA air-filtration system that was supposed to remove it.

Those were all expected, anticipated and not uncommon events in a hospital close to a major highway. Where there was trauma there was a busy ER and one of the reasons she'd come back here to her hometown. Reclaiming her life was the first reason. Working great trauma was the second. At least that was what she told herself as the crew swept past her.

What she hadn't expected to see was an emergency surgeon riding atop the gurney, straddling the patient, both of them covered in blood. Her limbs began to tremble and sweat popped out on her back. *Oh, man.* The heartbeat she usually kept calm with meditation now raced uncontrollably in her chest as she recognized the man behind the dirty scrubs. He'd aged little in three years and was as handsome as ever. A tightness in her abdomen surged to join the erratic heartbeat. Fierce intensity showed on his face and confidence she'd never seen in him before. His hair, dark brown with a tendency to curl, was a mess.

Those intense blue eyes blazed with a fire she'd never forgotten despite three years of separation.

"Get three units of whole blood going now. I need a central line placed and get OR on alert." Trauma surgeon and emergency doctor Chase Montgomery gave orders as the entourage rolled through the door. Staff scrambled to the first trauma room that had been set up for the arrival of this patient.

Emily choked down her anxiety, shoving it aside in the face of a true emergency, and grabbed the cardiac leads, placed them on the patient so his heart could be monitored and placed the blood-pressure cuff on the only arm he had left. The trembling in her hands was likely not noticeable to the others, but to her it was. This wasn't who she was, a nervous nurse on the first day of work. Like there weren't ten years under her belt already. But *this* place. *This* man. Those were the things that made her tremble now. Thoughts of how they'd been together in the past made her quake.

"Get anesthesia in here. He has to be intubated now."

"There was just an overhead page, Chase. They've been called to a code on the floor." Liz, the charge nurse, supplied the answer, but picked up the phone on the wall. "I'll see if there's someone else who can help out."

"Page any surgeon overhead. I'll intubate, and someone else can do the IV placement. We need a central line right away."

"Got it." Liz made the call.

"IV set-up tray is ready, Doctor, but if you'd prefer to intubate first, I'll get that one ready." Though keeping her focus on the patient, Emily spoke in the direction of the doctor leading the situation. He stood with his back to her and was in the process of removing his lab coat when he froze.

Then spun.

Clearly astonished at her presence, he stared at her with his mouth open for a few seconds as he tried to force his mind to accept what his eyes were seeing.

Emily's stomach tightened again; her heart beat as erratically as the patient's. Chase had never looked better, and her heart was out of control. A look of stunned shock crossed his face for a second or two. His eyes opened wide, his jaw dropped and he jumped as if he'd been pinched. Only a few seconds of lapsed control, but she saw it, felt it in her chest. The depth of pain mixed with his surprise at seeing her would be etched in her mind forever. She'd done that to him. She'd caused the hurt he'd momentarily betrayed. Except for the shock on his face, he hadn't changed in the three years since they'd broken up. Since she'd walked away from him.

"Emily?" He took a halting step toward her then stopped. "What are you *doing* here?" His blue gaze raked her from top to toe as if his brain still couldn't comprehend what his eyes were telling him. "What happened to your hair?"

Before she could answer, what seemed like an army of people burst into the room and the focus returned to the critical patient in front of them. This was apparently the *entire* team of surgeons, from the senior fellow down to the first-year resident. At a teaching hospital staff seemed to move in large herds.

"Who called for a surgeon? We're here."

As the physician in charge, Chase forced his focus from Emily to the surgeon. "We need better IV access immediately. Can one of you put in a central line? Anesthesia's tied up, and I'll have to intubate." Chase whipped off the bloody lab coat he'd worn to the crash site and threw it into a corner of the room.

The most senior member of the group emerged and nodded to Chase. "Sure thing." He removed his lab coat and handed it to a student to hold.

"I'll assist, Doctor." Emily made the offer so she would be away from Chase's penetrating glare and the waves of hostile energy flowing off him to flood the room. There was enough tension in the room already without adding more fuel to the fire she'd not been prepared for. Even though she'd known it would come, she wasn't prepared for it on the first day. "I've got the tray ready."

"Okay. Great. I thought this was going to be something difficult," he said with a grin, and winked at Emily. Emily never knew whether to be relieved at the confidence of surgeons or shocked at their outrageous arrogance. "Hey, don't I know you? Didn't you work here a while back?" He, too, frowned, trying to make sense of his memory in the present situation.

"Yes, I did. Came back for more. Over here, Dr. Blaze." Emily motioned him to the opposite side of the patient, and he moved around to where she stood. Relief overwhelmed her that he only remembered her from being an employee, not the rest. Or, if he did, he had the good graces not to say anything.

"Dr. Blaze. Ha! I haven't been called that in years."

"I remember with you everything was an emergency, wasn't it? You flashed through rounds like your tail was on fire." Emily smiled and her peripheral vision caught the glare Chase threw her way.

"Oh, those were the days." He shook his head at the memory. "So what happened? He's missing an arm." He looked to Chase for answers.

"Trauma. Pinned under his truck. Had to amputate in the field." Chase supplied the information, reinforcing one of the highest rules in trauma care: a limb for a life.

Focus. That was what he needed right now—focus. Nothing mattered right now except saving this man's life. That was why he was there.

It didn't matter that he'd just had a bomb go off in the form of his ex-girlfriend appearing right in front of him in the middle of a trauma. He had to focus right now and ignore the kick in his pulse and the pain in his heart. He continued speaking to the surgeon, though he focused on aligning the patient's head in the correct position for putting in the airway tube.

"Once he's stable you can take him to OR and clean the arm up. It was pretty quick and dirty out there." As an emergency surgeon, he was called on to perform such procedures as well as his normal shifts in the ER.

Though he would sound like he was in control to the others, Emily heard the tension in his voice, noticed the hardness in his eyes and the twitch of a muscle in his jaw. Always had been giveaways to his mood. He was brittle, and her shoulders tensed, waiting for him to snap. At her. She deserved it for not warning him she was going to be working with him again. But she'd been too chicken to call him and hear the intimacy of his voice in her ear and remember how that had used to feel. Now she could see it would have been better for her to have had someone let him know.

"Gotcha." The chief surgeon turned to face Emily and accepted her assistance to don sterile garb.

"Liz, let's get him intubated. Has next of kin been notified?" As the leading doctor in this case, Chase directed the care and the flow of procedures. This was *his* patient and *his* case until he turned it over to another physician.

"Family's on the way in." Liz expertly opened the tray and prepared it for Chase.

"Let's get a line in this fellow, and you can get that blood into him, shall we?"

Though Emily had assisted in this procedure many times in her career as a nurse and had been a travel nurse in all manner of hospitals from small community centers to large teaching hospitals, she'd never had the added pressure of having her ex-boyfriend breathing down her neck. After a deep breath in, she let it out slowly, trying to calm her nerves, which had shot out of control. Why had she thought this was a good idea again? Facing fears and all that? What rot that was. Right now, on the edge of panic, she'd be happy to spend the rest of the shift hiding in a dark closet somewhere.

The procedure went as planned and as soon as the surgeon had secured the line with a few stitches she connected two pints of blood and opened the tubes full blast. The sooner she restored the depleted amount of blood the man had lost, the better his chances of survival.

The hum around her was comforting and familiar, even though some of the staff were strangers. As they moved past the trauma room she recognized people with whom she'd previously worked. Some excitedly waved to her; others waved, then a memory surfaced in their eyes and their smiles stiffened. Coming back here, she'd known it would be a risk to her privacy. Some people would only remember working with her; some would only remember what had happened to her.

Regardless, staff had jobs to do, and everyone seemed to be able to do it while talking about mundane issues like the weather or the upcoming sailboat races in the Chesapeake Bay. Now that the most emergent procedures had been carried out, they could take a breath and relax a bit.

Except for Emily. She could never relax. That word was no longer part of her vocabulary, and she didn't anticipate it ever being again. Some days it was all she could do to focus on her work and not let the demons hiding behind every curtain or closet door terrorize her. Though three years had passed since the incident that had changed her life, there were times it felt just like yesterday.

"Liz, do you want me to call OR again?" She made the offer, hoping she could leave the room and make the call at the desk, give herself a bit of physical distance between her and Chase and draw a deep breath. Since the trauma she'd suffered three years ago, she had difficulty facing crowded rooms and tight spaces. Add stairwells and dark hallways to the list. Anxiety had been her dark shadow, and she hadn't managed to kick it. Yet. Now, with Chase in close proximity, that dark demon had a choke hold on her and wasn't letting go. She swallowed, trying to force down the memory of hands closing around her throat, assaulting her body. She coughed once, forcing her throat open, and clenched her hands into fists.

"No, you stay here and monitor the patient. I'm going to call them back. Their transport team should have been here by now." She reached for the phone just as the corner of a gurney poked through the entrance to the room.

"We're here. No worries." One of the large men in scrubs held up his hands in surrender. He looked around the room. "Looks like you're still at it. We'll wait outside."

"No, take him now. I'll go along and give you a report on the way." Chase spoke to the surgeon. "He was involved in a rollover crash that threw him from the wreckage, pinned his left arm beneath the vehicle." He shrugged into his crumpled lab coat as the crew prepared the patient for transport.

"You must have gotten *there* pretty quick to get him *here* in time." The surgeon also donned his lab coat and straightened his collar as if he were preparing to go to his office rather than about to perform a complicated emergency surgery. The man must have nerves of steel.

"I went in the chopper. That helped." Chase took a deep breath, as if some of that memory bothered him, but she knew better. Nothing really bothered him. Not back then and probably not ever. He must be part duck, because everything just seemed to roll right off him. Not that he was cold or unfeeling; he just compartmentalized things. And she'd been shoved into a compartment that hadn't fit her after the incident, and it was one she couldn't remain in and survive. She'd broken out and run until she couldn't run any longer.

Running never solved anything, but she'd had to figure that out on her own.

"Good times. Did you bring the limb with you? We might be able to reattach it. Vascular team is stellar." Chase nodded to the heavy-duty cooler on a counter behind him and one of the transport team picked it up, put it beneath the gurney. Both men grabbed opposing ends of the stretcher and moved with the patient toward the elevators, with the entire surgical team streaming down the hall behind them. Their voices faded into the distance as Chase and the surgeon continued their dialogue.

"Emily? You okay?" Liz asked, as she began to clean the room, preparing it for the next patient. "Hey, there. You okay?"

"What?" She blinked, took a breath and realized she was staring after Chase. "Oh, yes. I'm good." To hide her discomfiture, she shoved a handful of used gauze dressings into the hazardous waste can. Good thing it was a big one. "I can clean the room if you have other things to do." She'd appreciate a moment alone after the shocking experience she'd just had, and she didn't mean the patient.

"Let's work together. That's how we do things around

here." Liz carefully picked up the needles from the tray and disposed of them in the puncture-proof container hanging on the wall. "You might be used to getting all the crappy jobs as a traveler, but here we treat travel nurses the same as permanent staff." She smiled at Emily. "Right off the bat you caught a tough case, so I'll try to give you some lighter patients for the rest of the day. Not a guarantee, but I'll try."

"Thanks." It gave Emily a surge of warmth in her chest to hear the unit philosophy hadn't changed since she'd last worked there. She smiled and felt a little bit lighter as she talked, a little more at home.

Together they finished tidying the room and preparing it for the next patient. There would always be a next patient, a next trauma, a next disaster, and they had to be prepared for every kind that rolled through their doors.

"So, the next question is that you seem to have recognized Dr. Montgomery. Am I right?" Liz had the skills of a trained ER nurse and no denial was going to get past her. She'd see right through it. "And some other staff seemed to know you."

"Yes. I used to work here with him. Three years ago." She looked down and tried to control the beating of her heart. At one time Chase had been her heart, her life and her future, but that had all changed when she'd walked away from him. Though she hadn't wanted to, she'd had to. "And there are other staff I know, too." Some had saved her life in this very ER.

"There seemed to be more than just a recognition of a former coworker, though." Compassion and curiosity hung in her words, as if she suspected what Emily was going to tell her.

"There was." How much to tell without giving away her life story? "We dated at one time. But it was a while ago."

What seemed a lifetime ago. No need to tell Liz they had been a serious couple before she'd been brutally attacked by a serial rapist and had been forced to radically change her life. Without Chase.

That stopped Liz. "Is it going to be an issue between you? I mean, are you going to be able to work with him? He's one of our finest doctors and if you can't get along with him, we'll have to reconsider your contract, maybe place you in another unit or something."

"Oh, no. I'll be fine. I'll be nothing except professional with him. I'm certain he'll be cordial, as well." Work had always come first with him. His career, his work, saving lives had always come before her.

"If you're certain." Liz jerked the curtain back as the last gesture of room readiness. "I will trust you to let me know if that changes."

"I will. I appreciate it." She shoved her hands into the pockets of her scrubs. She was an adult, and she would behave like one. Chase would probably just ignore her, anyway. Her brother had told her he'd been dating other women, *many* other women, so she was probably nothing but a blip on his radar at this point. "Now, what else do we have to do? I need to keep busy." Keeping her hands busy kept her mind busy and prevented her thoughts from taking her down the rough road of her past and the never-ending trail of what-ifs and if-onlys.

"There'll be plenty to keep you occupied here. This isn't a big hospital, but it sure is a busy one. As you know, we're right off the interstate, so we have trauma on a daily basis." Liz led the way to the nurses' station and Emily followed, eager to get on with her orientation. "If trauma's not your bag now, by the end of your assignment it certainly will be.

CHAPTER TWO

CHASE RETURNED TO the ER, kept his pace slow, his thoughts on his work and tried to remain calm, despite the churning in his gut. But the second he saw Emily take a seat at the nurses' station, his nerves shot into overdrive. What the *hell* was she doing here? In *his* ER? Not that it was really his ER, but it was his by default, since she'd left it to pursue a travel-nursing stint.

She'd packed up her apartment, stuffed everything in a storage unit and driven away, not caring that he'd suffered in a way she couldn't imagine. Had she blamed him? He didn't know because she'd never said, but he damned sure blamed himself for not protecting her and for not being what she'd needed. Whatever that was. Seeing her now brought up so many feelings he'd buried, having been unable to work through them at the time. He didn't need this now. He didn't need it ever.

She was the last thing he'd expected to see after coming in on the trauma chopper today. When she spoke, the tone of her voice, the soft, dewy vibrations cut him to the core, as if only yesterday she'd meant something to him. He hadn't been expecting her and hadn't prepared himself to see her there. Surely *someone* could have told him she was coming. He could have prepared, could have hardened his heart and his emotions against the first meeting, put up boundaries, not been broadsided, unprepared. He'd never imagined she'd come back here where it had all begun for them.

That was probably the biggest shock. She'd come back to where he was when there were other hospitals in the area. So why here? And why *now*? That was a puzzle he intended to solve and then get on with his life. There was an answer for everything, and he was going to find this one.

When she'd left for her travel assignment he hadn't expected to ever see her again. Their breakup had been bitter, doubly so due to the assault and rape he hadn't been able to protect her from. That was the sorest spot, which had never healed.

He blamed himself.

She'd been unprotected because of him and had nearly died as a result, sustaining permanent scars inside and out. He hadn't known how to help her afterward, had been unable to help her, and when he'd been unable to face his own failure he'd backed away from her. He'd meant to give her some time and space, but not for all eternity. Her brother was a good friend, but Danny hadn't mentioned she was coming back. Maybe Danny hadn't wanted to upset him or had thought perhaps he'd moved on, and she no longer mattered to him.

He *had* moved on when she'd burned him back then. He'd been hurt and angry and hadn't been able to cope with his failure and the loss of her. Guilt had nearly eaten him alive. He'd dated women left and right. Sometimes for fun, sometimes for sex and sometimes for spite. Some had been gorgeous, some had been entertaining and some for no reason at all, other than convenience.

Unfortunately, none of them had been Emily. No woman had ever measured up to what he and Emily had

had before the event that had fractured their lives. Neither of them would be the same again. Obviously. The incident hadn't just happened to her, it had nearly destroyed him, as well. It had taken him years to crawl back to where he felt human again and now, in an instant, everything had imploded.

The moment he'd heard her voice in the trauma room his soul had reacted with utter joy and then utter sorrow. Her voice and those big, expressive eyes of hers hadn't changed and his body had reacted to her with vigor. Embarrassing in a room full of people in an emergency, but he'd never been able to control himself around her before, so why should it be different now?

He closed the door to the charting room with disgust and sat down at the computer terminal to write up his notes from the morning's trauma. The coffee sat untouched beside him, and the words blurred together on the screen. Nothing made sense at the moment, and he pressed his fingertips to his eyes, wanting to rip out the image of her standing there with all that spiky hair, looking so different yet much the same and so very beautiful.

Why had Emily come back?

Seeing Chase right off the bat this morning had shaken her, torn up the defenses she'd worked so hard to build. She'd hidden it well, or so she thought, from the others, but now the shakes had set in. She hadn't expected to see him first thing, first trauma of the day, but that was life.

What had she thought when she'd returned to this hospital? Had she just come here to test herself for some stupid reason? She had just thought she was going to waltz in there and never see him, never have him recognize her despite the changes to her hair, her body, her life? She snorted in self-disgust. Apparently, that was what she'd hoped, whether it had been conscious or unconscious in its creation. Reclaiming her life wasn't going to be as easy as it sounded.

If she were being honest with herself, she wanted to see him, wanted to see if there was any spark left between them. She'd healed so many parts of her life, but this one had been the biggest wound to her heart and her soul and it had been left cracked, bleeding and raw. So she'd come home to make amends with Chase and get over him for good. One way or another, it had to be decided or she couldn't get on with her life. She was stuck. Stuck on Chase.

Denial was a wonderful thing, which helped people cope with tragic situations. It also helped them be stupid a little too long sometimes. Like her. She'd needed it in the beginning, when things had been very bad. Over the years she'd thought she'd kicked her dependence on it, had been able to stand up on her own. She'd changed her life and had thought she'd changed who she was on the inside, too.

Chase had seen right through her little masquerade to the heart of her the second he'd leveled those surprised laser blue eyes of his on her. That had rattled her as nothing had in three years. Over that time she'd thought she'd forget about them, about him, and move on, the way she knew he'd done. She'd thought she'd been prepared to see him, to be coworkers again. But her plan had backfired the moment she'd seen him. *Kapow!*

The guilt and somehow the bitter relief of their breakup had hurt and rocked her world, but she'd been able to crawl out of the hole finally.

Nothing had rocked her world the way it had when his eyes had met hers this morning.

Nothing.

And now she had to reconsider this assignment, this idea of hers to return to her home and make a new life, to make a place for herself again. Her family was here. Her friends were here. And her memories were here. Maybe Liz was right. Maybe she needed to be assigned to a different unit so she didn't have to work with Chase every day. Was the answer just to avoid him and enjoy the rest of her assignment? She could still catch up with friends, with family, visit old haunts like the James River, the Chesapeake Bay and enjoy socializing again. That sounded like a fine plan.

For someone else.

Although she'd left the area after her assault, she didn't consider herself a coward to run away from things or run away from people. This return to her home was the last part of her healing, of coming full circle to where things had begun, and to come face-to-face with her fears, her anxiety, and spit in the eyes of the demons that had haunted her for three years.

It was time. She was ready. It was the last step to recovery. Today, she'd stepped into the pond, and she'd see if she could swim again.

A month ago, when she'd been talking to her nurse recruiter, the idea had sounded like the right idea at the time. Go home to the Tidewater area of eastern Virginia, reconnect with her roots, be near her family for the fall and spend the holidays together. Her parents had been thrilled, and it had all seemed a good idea. Her brother, Danny, a firefighter, seemed to think it was a good idea, too. Time to come home and reclaim her life. Full circle.

That was the trouble with brilliant ideas. They always seem good at the time you cooked them up, but then, when the bacon hit the pan, you needed to expect some sizzle and smoke.

There was definitely sizzle when it came to Chase Montgomery. Lots of sizzle. That hadn't changed, but now she wasn't certain she was prepared to face it, to face him knowing she had been responsible for their breakup.

"You ready?" Liz asked, interrupting her train of thought.

"Sure. What are we doing now?"

"Computer training. That's probably new since you were here. Half the staff still don't know how to use it. Training has been a real pain."

"I've used a couple of different kinds of software, so maybe this one will be something I already know."

"Wouldn't that be great? Save us both some headaches."

Emily reacquainted herself with the computer system, and how the charting requirements had changed since she'd previously worked there. Then the moment she'd dreaded happened.

She came face-to-face with Chase in the hallway by the staff lounge. Alone.

"Oh. Hi there." Flustered, she tucked a strand of hair behind her ear. Or she tried to. It was an old habit she hadn't dropped when she'd cut her hair short. The last time she'd seen Chase her hair had been halfway down her back. Now it didn't even cover her ears.

"Hi." Chase looked as if he was surprised to see her as well. He cleared his throat, and his gaze skittered away from hers. "Uh…you cut your hair."

"Yes. Yes, I did." How awkward was this? *Very!*

"It looked better long." He looked at her as if remembering or trying to remember how it had looked on her before.

"Yes, well. Suits my lifestyle now." She tried to walk around him at the same time he tried to walk around her, and they ended up bouncing off each other.

"Sorry."

"Sorry." She stomped a foot. "This is so annoying."

"What is? Running into your old lover or being told you look better with long hair?" Chase took a step back and paused, interested in hearing the answer. He crossed his arms and waited for her, knowing he wasn't going to like any reason she had. Why should he? She was the one interrupting the status quo of his life. That didn't come without risk or consequences. Did she think he was just going to accept her unexpected presence with open arms and forget how she'd destroyed his life? She was the one who'd walked away, not him. If he admitted his part, that he'd let her go, that he hadn't chased her down and made her stay, he'd have to look too closely at things best left in the past. At least, that was what he felt right now.

"Well, both, but mostly running into you when I hadn't expected it." Okay. There it was, out in the air between them. The honesty he could appreciate.

"Imagine my surprise when I saw you in the trauma room." He raised his brows and looked down at her. In the past he'd considered her height cute. She was short, but she'd hit him at just the right place when they'd been wrapped up in each other. He blew out a breath at the unexpected memory.

"There was no way to avoid it."

"Seriously? I had no advanced warning. You could have called me." Dammit. Someone should have called him and let him know she was coming.

"And what? Warned you I was going to be working in the ER and *might* run into you? For all I knew, you weren't even here, or were married with six kids." Big. Fat. Lie. She still had friends in the hospital, and they'd let her know he was still there. Still single. Still hot. *Very hot.*

"I see." He stiffened, and his eyes went icy. "Danny could have told me."

"Why? We're old news, right? Now we're just two professionals working together, and the rest doesn't matter, does it?" What mattered was that her heart was palpitating, her breath was tight in her throat, and her legs didn't want to move. Old news. *Right*. Denial was her BFF.

"Yes. Well. I can be professional, and I'm certain you will be, too." The ice hadn't left his veins, but at least he was being civil. That was more than she should expect from him. And there was nothing he could do about her presence. She was a good nurse, so he'd have to keep his personal reasons to himself. They had no bearing here.

"Of course. I expected nothing less. I'm sorry. I should have gotten word to you."

"Yes, you should have. It would have been simple courtesy."

At least she'd apologized and some of his irritation dissolved. Maybe he could overlook it, maybe not, but it was a situation he was going to have to deal with.

"Again. Sorry." She glanced away. "I was going to grab some coffee then head back out there."

"Pot's on the right. Creamer and sugar in cupboard above." Dammit. Why had he said that? He didn't care how she took her coffee any longer. Why had he told her that when he hadn't meant to?

"You remember how I take my coffee?" Surprise showed in her eyes. Blinking those big blue eyes of hers, she held his gaze for the first time since he'd seen her again. What was she looking for? Hell, what was *he* looking for? The past revealed in each other's eyes? Hardly.

"I never forgot." He paused for another second and took a long slow look over her. "Anything." With that declaration he pushed away before he said something truly stupid and headed into the main part of the ER. How in the world was he going to get through three months with her underfoot, under his skin? Had he just lied to her *and* himself by telling her he could be a professional? The way he felt now was nothing close to it. What he felt was…ripped open. Raw in a way he hadn't allowed himself to feel in the years since she'd broken him and left town.

He was a physician, an ER doctor and an emergency surgeon, and proud of what he'd accomplished in his career. He was a professional, and he saved the lives of trauma victims every day. That was why he was here in this hospital. But if he were being honest with himself, so was Emily. She was a damned good trauma nurse with excellent skills. The hospital had had a turnover of staff in the last few months, and they needed quality staff, hence the number of travel nurses presently in the hospital. Experience didn't come easily or without cost. He knew that, and he was forced to admit she'd worked damned hard for hers.

She also had the unfortunate, firsthand experience of being on the receiving end of a terrible trauma, which made her uniquely qualified to be doing the kind of work she did.

Not wanting to travel down that bumpy road again right now, he moved forward, moved toward the next patient, the next chart, the next issue in front of him, despite his memories wanting to drag him back into the past.

The day progressed more slowly in the afternoon. Staff came to him with more mundane issues that kept him busy, but he still felt as if he were walking through water up to his chest. Slowly, trudging along. The oppression of the past weighed heavily on his mind and his spirit.

"Dr. Montgomery? Chase?" The words eventually penetrated his brain that someone was calling to him.

"Yes?" He frowned as Liz and Emily stood beside him.

"I was going to introduce you to our new travel nurse, but I think you've met before, right?"

"Correct." That was the simplest, most unemotional way to present it. Dry.

"Okay. One less thing on the checklist to do." She gave an awkward smile. "I see. Sorry to bug you."

"No problem." Keeping all expression and emotion from his face was getting harder to do, and he felt himself gritting his teeth. Thankfully he had a good dental plan, because he would probably be doing that for the next three months.

"Actually, I had a question for Dr. Montgomery about a new patient." Emily spoke to Liz, but looked at Chase. Professional. Cool. Fine.

"Sure. What's up?" He could do it, too. Really. He leaned back in the desk chair and raised his hands over his head, waiting for her to speak.

"I'll catch you later," Liz said, and moved away.

Emily filled him in on the background of the patient in question. "This is a twenty-five-year-old male who is accustomed to being in the outdoors, hunting, fishing and camping. He's complaining of joint pain, fatigue, and general malaise. I'm going to put in a lab request for the usual workup, but I was wondering if we should test for Lyme disease as well."

Chase frowned as he thought about the details of the case and processed the facts. Concise, important symptoms, and a little detective work to boot. Smart, beautiful and still sexy as hell. Dammit. "Is he running a fever?"

"On and off for a few weeks, since his last camping trip in western Maryland." She didn't face him but stood beside him, facing the computer. "He also noticed a classic bull's-eye rash on his leg and got worried when it didn't resolve right away."

"That's ground zero for Lyme exposure." He nodded. "Go ahead and add the panel, but explain to him it's a two-part test and it will be a week before we get results."

"I will. Thank you, Doctor." She nodded, keeping her eyes downcast as she walked away.

So it was going to be the cool doctor-nurse relationship between them. He could do that, too. He watched as she walked away. Her body had changed since back then. There was something different about the way she walked, more confident, more sure of herself, and her posture was definitely more upright. She actually appeared to be a little taller than her five-foot-five, petite frame, which had fit him perfectly. Now he'd have to reconsider that. Not that there was going to be an opportunity for her to fit to his body anymore. *Ever.*

An hour later she approached again. He was still in the same position at the computer console, having gotten no further in his documentation. "Can you see this patient now? The possible Lyme guy?"

"Sure. Are labs back?"

"Yes. Chest X-ray, too."

"Let me have a look at them first." He clicked a few times, certain he was following the right pathway to the test results, but there was no X-ray. "It's not here. Are you sure you ordered the right tests on this patient?" Irritation crept into his voice, despite his desire to not react to her at all. "Being timely is important around here, Emily. We don't sit around—"

"Yes. I'm sure. I printed them up if you'd like to look at them the old-fashioned way." She gave a tight smile. "Might be easier for you."

"No." Focusing on the screen, he gave an irritated sigh,

then clicked and clicked again, with no better results. "Dammit."

With a sigh, Emily leaned over his shoulder and took the mouse from his right hand. "Let me see. Oh, you've got the wrong patient up, that's all." She masterfully clicked here and there and in seconds had the proper patient with the labs and X-ray reports side by side on the screen. "There you go. Easy."

He cast a baleful eye at her and really wanted to feel irritated, but the fact was he hated this computer system and had refused to spend the time to learn it properly. As soon as he did that, it would be changed to something else, so why bother?

"Show-off." The second he turned to glare at her he knew it was a mistake, making him grit his teeth again. The fragrance he'd never been able to get out of his mind filled his senses and images of her in his arms hit him like a ton of bricks. The memories came over him hard and fast. The body wash she loved to use in the shower, her long hair slicked back from her pretty face, the water sluicing down her body, over the curves of her breasts and hips. Jeez, his thoughts were inappropriate. So much for being a professional.

His gaze dropped to her mouth, as lush and full as he remembered it. The smile on her face froze as she met his gaze full on. Her pupils dilated, and he knew she was thinking the same thing. Would there be anything, any spark between them again? Could there be? Then she straightened and took a step back.

"Yes. Well. There they are, Doctor. I've used this system a few times at other hospitals. Pretty simple once you get to know it." She dropped her gaze and blew out a quick breath.

"I see." Clearly, she was not unaffected by his presence and not as cool as she pretended to be. But that was not his problem.

Nothing Emily Hoover did was his problem. Ever again.

CHAPTER THREE

THE SOUND OF raised voices generally got some attention, even in an ER full of chaos. This one was in relation to Emily's last patient of the day, who had come in thirty minutes ago. A woman, in her midforties, had said she'd tripped over her cat and hit her cheek on a doorknob. Emily had seen plenty of trips and falls and doorknob injuries, but this was not one of them. The woman had warned Emily her husband was going to be making an intoxicated appearance. He stumbled his way through the automatic doors right on cue.

"I don't care who you are—I'm going in there to see my wife." The man was a belligerent one, not used to a woman who had her own power and didn't care one whit about his. He was used to getting his way by bullying and it wasn't working, which only made his color go from pink to a florid red.

"Sir, your wife doesn't want to see you right now. You're drunk and—"

"The hell you say." Unable to stand up without swaying only added proof to her statement. Emily kept him in full view of the security camera so there would be plenty of evidence if needed later.

"I don't say. *She* says, and what she says goes. Got it?" Emily stood her ground, facing the large man dressed in hunting camo. This wasn't the first time she'd had to handle an upset family member, so she called on her years of ER experience to remain calm and keep the upper hand. She cast a glance at one of the staff members and nodded. It was a silent signal to notify Security they were needed in the ER immediately. Her job was to keep him distracted until they arrived.

"Get out of my way, bitch." The man reached out to grab Emily by the shoulder, obviously intending to shove her out of the way.

Emily had good reflexes and jumped back so he couldn't touch her, but Chase hurried over to her, putting himself between her and the drunk. The man was huge, and towered over Chase by a foot.

"Don't touch her." He spoke forcefully to the man and tried to calm his nerves at the sight of him reaching for Emily. "Don't touch any of our staff, or you'll be looking at assault charges." Chase didn't know if the words were penetrating the man's whiskey-soaked brain cells but he had to try.

"Like I care." He glared at Chase, but didn't move to touch him.

"Sir, I said your wife doesn't want to see you right now, and if you continue to resist, you'll be hauled out of here by Security." Emily spoke from beside Chase. She'd moved forward to stand beside him, providing a unified front with him. Other staff members eased closer. If the man lunged for Emily again, they could jump him without anyone getting hurt.

"You got no reason to keep me from my wife." The man was sweating, his face was red and he stunk to high heaven.

"Actually, we can. You can't be in here drunk. Security's on the way, and they're going to call the police to haul you off to jail." Chase experienced significant satisfaction that the situation was going to end without incident. Having Emily assaulted in front of him would not have been good. Just thinking about it brought back all sorts of horrid images he'd buried. Or so he'd thought.

"What? You can't have me arrested." The man started toward Emily again and tried to kick her, but she avoided his inaccurate jabs. Chase held his hands out to the sides and jumped to block him from getting any closer.

"Dr. Montgomery, he can't get to me. Don't worry," Emily said. She gave a quick grin in his direction, and his heart reacted against his will. That impish grin had never left his mind and, combined with the short, spiky hair, she looked like a little fairy with a bad attitude.

Two muscled security team members, dressed in black, arrived and joined Chase. "We'll take it from here."

"He's all yours. I have patients to wrap up before the end of shift," Emily said, and stepped around the man, but he took a swipe at her and missed. Again. Nerves calming, Chase watched as Emily easily avoided the man's giant hand and wondered what she'd been doing to gain such reflexes.

"You little bitch. I'm gonna get you for this."

"Is that a threat? Are you threatening her?" Chase stepped forward, all amusement gone. "I think you've just threatened a staff member here. In front of witnesses and on security cameras. We'll add that to the trespassing charges already on the list."

"Oh, man." He began to whine and snivel. "I just wanna see my wife." Stomping his foot, he looked like a petulant toddler held between the security guards.

Chase approached and put his face as close to the drunk as was tolerable given the fumes emanating off him. Fortunately, it was a no-smoking hospital or they could have gone up in flames. "I believe *you're* the reason she's in the ER in the first place, are you not?"

Pause. "Yes."

"Did you drive here?" Chase asked.

"If it's any of your business, yes." He tried to spit at Chase, who moved deftly out of range.

"Fellows, let the police know to add impaired driving to the list."

"Got it." They hauled the man out of the ER to await the police.

"Are you okay? Really?" Despite himself, Chase moved toward Emily, concerned that the threat might trigger memories of her assault again, the way they were starting to in him. No matter what he felt for her now, he didn't want to see her hurt by anyone. This time he'd been able to help out, even though it had been a small effort.

"Nah, I'm good. I have new ninja reflexes. He didn't even get close." Demonstrating her technique, she jumped around in front of him looking quite like a ninja in scrubs.

She gave that grin again and his heart now seemed to have no immunity against it. "I see." He cleared his throat and clamped down his anxiety for her safety.

That reflex hadn't gone away just because they weren't a couple anymore. Of course, he probably would have reacted the same no matter what staff member had been involved in the kerfuffle. At least, that was what he told himself.

Turning away from the scene, Emily rolled her shoulders a few times then picked up her clipboard. "Okay. Dr. Montgomery, can you see this patient now?"

"Uh, sure." He stepped closer, more comfortable with the doctor-nurse role. "Is this the wife?"

"Yes. Superficially, she looks roughed up a bit, nothing serious, other than needing to get away from her husband." Emily shook her head. "Can't say I blame her."

"You think he beat her up?" Anger flashed hot and fast inside him. Women and children were precious, and were to be protected, not used as punching bags by drunken men who couldn't control their tempers.

"She won't cop to it, says she tripped, fell into a door. It's mostly the face. Black eye on the right, swollen shut, cheek bruised and swollen. Not sure if it's fractured, but it won't hurt to have an X-ray of it."

He followed her without comment to the patient room and when Emily held the curtain back, Chase's stomach clenched. The image of the woman before him sickened him. She was in her midforties. Her face was so swollen she looked as if she had been in a car accident and it instantly reminded him of the night he'd seen Emily in a similar condition. Trying to remain in that professional space, he took a quick breath and stepped close to the gurney. Emily was right. He didn't even need the X-rays to know she'd been beaten up. In their line of work they'd become unfortunate experts on the topic.

"Mrs. Billings? I'm Dr. Montgomery. Nurse Hoover has made some recommendations for your treatment, and I'm inclined to agree with her." He trusted her nursing experience, if nothing else.

"Like what?" She turned a defeated gaze to him. The sound of her voice was slow and thick. She'd probably bitten her tongue during the assault.

"Facial X-rays, possibly a CAT scan of your head to look for fractures in the sinuses and the left side of your face." He moved closer, and she jumped. "Sorry, didn't mean to startle you." More carefully, he approached her and focused on keeping everything slow, his voice soft.

She'd obviously been conditioned to watch out for any sudden movements her husband made.

"Go ahead." She closed her eyes, as if trying to shut out the world. "I don't care."

"Are you in pain?"

She nodded and tears began to overflow. "Don't be nice to me, Doc. I can't take it." She sniffed. "I don't know what it's like."

"Then I'll try harder to be mean," he said, and received a crooked smile.

"Thanks."

He looked at Emily, who looked pale and a little wide-eyed. "I'll get right on those orders, Doctor." Then she turned back to the patient and the moment was gone, if it had been there at all. Maybe he'd only imagined the haunted look on her face as she'd watched her patient.

Avoiding Chase and the look on his face was her goal. Seeing this woman had brought back memories for both of them that neither of them cared to have. Caring for this woman was her job, and she would do it well, but making eye contact with Chase would be her undoing. She had to avoid it. Like her patient, she couldn't deal with his compassion for her pain. What she needed to do was keep busy and focused on her work. The rest would eventually go away. It always did. Situations like this brought everything back to slam her right in the gut when she wasn't looking.

Trying to stop the trembling in her hands, she prepared the lab tubes and labeled them appropriately, but her mind was elsewhere.

Night, being alone in the dark, was the toughest. Night was when the shadows darkened in her mind and the whispers of her attacker infiltrated her barriers. *Bitch. I'm gonna get you, bitch.* Sometimes all it took was hearing that word *bitch* to send her all the way back to that dark awful night.

She applied the tourniquet to Mrs. Billings's arm and inserted the needle into the vein. Emily swallowed hard against the sudden dryness in her mouth. She filled each tube the way she was supposed to and applied a small dressing to the tiny puncture site of the left arm. Focused. Clinical.

Emily placed the tubes filled with blood for testing into a zippered lab bag for transport. After setting them in the lab pick-up rack, she realized her heart hadn't settled down and the tightness in her chest hadn't eased. Was it Chase? Was it the husband? Was it this patient? Maybe all of it combined in such a short time worked together to rob her of her strength.

Making her way to the supply room, she checked to make sure she was alone then removed her lab coat, placed a towel on the floor, sat cross-legged on it and closed her eyes.

There was a place she liked to go mentally when stressed and it was a place from her past where she'd been happy, walking alone on the sand at Virginia Beach, feeling the warmth of the sun on her skin, the salt on the breeze and the coarse sand on her feet.

This was the place where she let go of stress, released it to the ocean waves and found some peace.

Until Chase walked into the supply room.

"What are you doing?" He stopped short just inside the doorway.

Startled, she opened her eyes. The serenity that had been on her face vanished and it was his fault. Dammit. She'd looked so peaceful for a second, and he'd ruined it.

"I *was* meditating." She blinked a few times, as if coming back to herself from wherever she had been.

"Now? In the middle of the shift?"

"Yes. I'm entitled to breaks. Several, in fact, over the course of twelve hours. What I do with them is my business." Closing her eyes again, she tried to ignore him, but it was impossible.

"Yes, that's true." He squatted down beside her, too close for her senses. "You never used to meditate." Obvious irritation showed in the frown between her delicate eyebrows and the downward turn of her mouth. Not that he blamed her.

"I never used to do a lot of things." She looked up at him, held his gaze, almost challenging him. "I've acquired some new skills."

"Like your new ninja reflexes? Are you taking karate or something?" He'd never seen her move so fast. That had impressed him.

"Not karate. If I had used karate I'd have taken out his knee first, but you got in front of me."

"Judo?" He really didn't know about martial arts and had just exhausted his knowledge.

"Hardly. In judo, I would have—"

"Whatever. Clearly, you're an expert now." And he'd had no clue.

"No. Just determined." There was an aura of steel about her now. And, yes, determination showed in her eyes. That was the difference he'd been sensing in her.

"To what?" He really wanted to know the answer to that. Genuine curiosity had been roused in him and for the first time today he could set aside the pain.

Without answering the question, she unfolded her legs and stood. "Did you come in here for something or just to annoy me?"

"I saw you come in here and after the day's events I

thought you looked a little off." That was okay. Looking after a coworker?

"Off? No. I'm fine." Turning away from him, she began to scan the shelves as if looking for something. "Gauze, suture materials, IV supplies over here. Good to know." She took a step to the next shelving unit. "GI supplies over here—oh, look, enemas. Never know when you need to get rid of some—"

"Stop it. You're not fine. If you're meditating in the middle of a shift, that must mean you're upset about something. Possibly nearly getting assaulted not long ago?" He let the question hang in the air between them.

She gave him a glare then kept scanning. "Maybe we need to order extra-large enemas for special cases." The glare she leveled on him left no doubt as to who she would use them on.

"Emily." Chase intended to make her face him, make her turn around, and placed a hand on her shoulder. Then squealed like a girl and nearly dropped to his knees in pain. "Augh!"

"Don't touch me, Chase." Again, her speed defied logic. He had been unprepared for her ability to take his wrist in her hand, apply pressure and leverage to the point of pain, yet she hadn't batted an eyelid. In fact, she looked calmer than she had since he'd entered the room. The control in her eyes impressed him and maybe scared him a little.

"Okay, okay, okay. Let go. *Let go.* Ow. *Ow.* I have to do surgery with that hand." She released him and the relief was great.

"Unless you want to have both hands in casts, don't ever try to touch me again." The calm, serious look on her face was something he never wanted to see aimed at him again, as if she were contemplating squishing an insect.

He shook his hand, grateful she hadn't really wanted to hurt him or it could have gotten ugly. Baffled, he looked at her as if seeing her for the first time, and maybe he was. Giving her a little space, he took a step back. "Where'd you learn all that stuff?" That was the change in her body he hadn't been able to identify before. She was muscular and toned in a way that wasn't from a weekly aerobics class. Yowza, she was strong.

Now she faced him fully, the brunt of her anger unleashed on him. "'Stuff'? Seriously?" Though half a foot shorter than he, the power of her was unbelievable and gloriously arousing. "That 'stuff' saved my life more than once. That 'stuff', as you call it—" she tossed her head "—has kept me sane for the last three years, and that *'stuff'* allows me sleep at night."

She nearly trembled with rage, and he could see it unfold within her. Her blue eyes sparkled, her face was flushed and pink, her chest rose and fell quickly. She was beautiful, and he did not want to see it, to feel anything for her, to be the recipient of her rage. But he couldn't help himself. He stood there in awe for a few seconds before he could speak.

"*Are* you okay?" His voice was a hoarse whisper that he barely recognized as his own. "Seriously?"

Then Emily blinked a few times, shook herself and let out a long, slow breath. "I'm fine. The meditation helped and now I'm ready to go out there and see if my lab results are back yet."

She tried to move past him, but he placed his hand on her arm. She stopped, looked at his hand then up at his face, calm and cool. Hastily, Chase extricated his hand.

"If you wish to continue to do surgery without having it yourself, I suggest you don't lay a hand on me again. *Ever.*"

"Sorry." Point made.

"I'll let you know about the labs as soon as they're back."

"O...*kay*." Reaching out, he opened the door and watched Emily walk away.

CHAPTER FOUR

TREMBLING SUBSIDING, Emily returned to the nurses' station and logged onto the computer, pulled up the lab results, reviewed them and clicked the print key. She would have to return to Chase, Dr. Montgomery, as she needed to remember to notify him of these results. The woman had obvious issues with her husband, but she had deeper problems, too, and it showed clearly in her lab results.

"Dammit, I don't want to talk to him anymore today," she grumbled aloud.

"And who would that be?" Liz asked, and plopped down in a chair beside her.

"Oh!" She whirled. "I thought I was by myself."

"In this place? Never." She patted Emily on the arm. "Now, tell me how you are and who you don't want to talk to. I came to check on you after the incident, but you disappeared for a while."

"Yeah. I was taking a few deep breaths in the supply room." No harm in admitting that, regardless of what Chase thought. "A little decompression."

"I see. Good." Liz nodded. "And the rest?"

With a sigh and a downward turn of her mouth Emily leaned back in the chair. "I've got labs to review with Dr. Montgomery, but I don't want to talk to him right now."

"Why not?" Liz held out her hand, and Emily gave the

lab reports to her. She took a few seconds to scan the numbers, automatically interpreting. "Everything looks good."

"Next page. Hematology."

"Oh, I see. Anemia and indications of infection. You're wondering if she has an underlying pathology you'll have to discuss with him."

"Yes." Thankfully, Liz understood. Maybe she would talk to Chase.

"I don't understand, though. Did he say or do something to you that upset you? He seemed impressed with how you handled the drunk husband."

"Really?" Now, that surprised her. He'd never been impressed about anything she'd ever done. Or at least he'd never admitted it.

"Yes. If I didn't know any better, I'd say he was concerned for you. But then he turned around and was the same old Chase."

"Same old Chase? What do you mean?" Despite her resolve, she was curious. After all, three years had passed since they'd seen one another and although her brother was good friends with him, he'd respected her boundaries and not mentioned Chase. Maybe she could surreptitiously get some information on Chase and it would satisfy the curiosity that had been plaguing her for the last year. Was he the same as she'd remembered?

"He's a regular guy—fun, friendly—but when it's time to be serious, he is."

Emily gaped. "Chase? *Fun?* Since when? He was never fun." She clamped her mouth shut and a knowing light entered Liz's eyes. "He was serious most of the time. Work came before everything else."

"I thought there was something serious between you two. You didn't just date a few times, did you?"

Keeping secrets was apparently not her forté, and she

shouldn't look forward to a career in the international espionage field. Damn. Maybe Liz could keep a secret.

"It was a long time ago." But was it really?

"Not that it's any business of mine, but it doesn't seem like business is over between you two. If the air needs to be cleared for you to work together, then I'd suggest having a chat with him." She sighed. "I'd suggest it to anyone who was having a difficult working relationship. If needed, there's always mediation."

"Mediation? No. We were done three years ago. And it was a bitter breakup."

"I'm sorry, Emily. It's none of my business, like I said, but if you ever need to talk, I can listen and it won't go anywhere." She had the calm eyes and demeanor of a true leader.

"Thanks, but I just need to pull myself together and be an adult about it." She'd put her big-girl panties on a long time ago. They just needed a little straightening now and then.

"Okay. The offer stands." She handed the papers back to Emily. "And I think Chase should see those right away." She nodded over Emily's shoulder.

"I should see what?" Face serious, he moved closer. The cologne he wore hadn't changed and it caught her by surprise. She'd loved that on him. Then.

"Labs here indicate some infection and something going on with her hematology." She shrugged, looked away and placed the printout on the counter in front of him so there was no accidental touching of skin to skin.

Without touching the papers, he leaned over and read them, nodding and focusing on the numbers in front of him, then turned his attention to her. "So what do you think we should do?"

"Me? You're the doctor. You should examine her and

then decide, but it appears she's losing blood somewhere." She stiffened at being put on the spot. "Although she didn't complain of any abdominal pain, and we were more concerned about her head trauma, it's possible she took a few hits to the abdomen and either her spleen or liver is leaking."

Just then the alarms in Mrs. Billings's room began to chime in earnest. Emily looked at the monitor beside her at the station displaying the vital signs in bold green numbers.

"What?"

"BP taking a nosedive and pulse shot up." She looked with concern at Chase and met his gaze full on. "She's in trouble."

They all raced into the room just in time to see the patient's eyes roll back in her head, and she lost consciousness. "Dammit," Chase cursed, and he rarely did that in front of a patient, no matter what the circumstance. "Call a code."

Emily hit the specially designed button on the wall behind the patient's head while Liz ran for the crash cart, the large tool chest on wheels housing lifesaving equipment.

People began arriving in droves to assist with the code. Thankfully, in a code situation no one was ever alone. Chase was in charge and ran the operation, but Emily was next in command and delegated tasks to other staff members if she wasn't able to perform them herself.

"Let's give her some fluids, wide open," Chase instructed, "then epinephrine IV push." He kept his gaze on the monitor, watching everything the heart did.

Emily didn't have to call for it as Liz had it prepared in a few seconds and handed it to her. Pulling the cap off, she connected the needleless system and pushed the medicine in as quickly as possible. The patient's heart rate suddenly paused, then dropped dramatically.

Chase whipped off the stethoscope from around his neck and listened to the patient's abdomen, and then used his hands to palpate it.

"How's her belly?"

"Rigid. Think you're right, Nurse Hoover. She's got a cracked liver and is bleeding into her abdomen. Call OR and tell them we're on the way up now. No time to wait. I'll have to operate, but call the surgical team for backup."

"Now I wish I'd hit him," she muttered beneath her breath, and jerked the receiver off the wall.

"What?"

"Nothing. Got it." She dialed and informed the OR of the situation of an emergency patient coming their way.

Staff scrambled to get her to the OR. Emily trotted along next to the stretcher as the crew moved down the hall to the OR, which was on the same floor but through a maze of hallways and double doors.

"There's something wrong in your abdomen, Jenny, so Dr. Montgomery is going to operate on you." She stroked the woman's hair. Sweat had popped out on her face and neck. Emily knew it was from shock and the compensating mechanisms her body was engaging in. The heart raced to make up for in rate what it lacked in output, due to low blood volume.

And then Mrs. Billings was gone. Emily handed her over to the pre-op nurses. Watching through the slight opening in the doors, she watched Chase approach the stainless-steel sinks, pull on a hair cover, mask, and begin to scrub. He wore the green, sterile scrubs required in the OR and was ready to roll.

Back in the day she'd used to love watching him scrub, knowing he was entering a world all his own in surgery, knowing he was going to drag a patient back from the edge of death.

Back then he'd been her superhero. Saving everyone and everything.

Only he'd failed her when she'd needed him the most. Nothing in life had ever disappointed her more. Time had helped her realize he was just a man and no cape could turn him into what she'd needed. But right now that man was going to bust his butt trying to save this woman. If nothing else, she had to respect him for that.

The remainder of the day passed with much less fuss than the first part of it. A few coughs, colds and possible flu filtered in, but her mind was never far from thoughts of Chase and the work he was doing on their patient.

At the end of shift Emily gave in to mental and physical exhaustion, allowing it to wash over her as she exited the building out into the staff parking lot. Fortunately, it wasn't a long walk.

This was the kind of situation that could lead to an assault on a woman who was not prepared the way Emily was now. Women left their jobs after long hours, eager to get home, their senses and muscles weakened by their work, not paying attention to the immediate surroundings. And alone. That was a sure setup for an attack.

Now Emily was different and more prepared than she'd ever been. Though exhausted, her senses, her self-protective instincts she'd honed over the years surged within her, brewing just under the surface, reaching out into the night, as if sentient. Sounds came to her from the twilight. The abrasive whirring of a cicada attracted her attention to the tops of the trees. Crickets trilled from the grass along the edge of the parking lot. A flock of pigeons overhead swooped past in search of a roosting place for the night.

A lone seagull hung on an updraft long enough to decide whether she was edible or not.

All familiar, comforting sounds.

Then footsteps crunched on the gravel behind her. Staff left the building at intervals, heading to their vehicles. *These* steps were deliberate and rapidly approaching her.

Without thinking, she dropped her bag and took a defensive posture, arms at the ready, prepared to defend herself. When she recognized the person approaching her she relaxed her stance, but her insides remained tense and jiggling for another reason.

Chase approached, still in the green scrubs, mask dangling from his neck and a grim look on his face. He must have news of their patient or he wouldn't be there.

"What are you doing out here?"

"I wanted to catch you before you left."

"How is she?" She didn't even have to ask. She knew why he was there.

"She's going to make it, but it was touchy for a while. Had to give her six units of blood. Livers are messy, as you know." And then he grinned. He was exhilarated by the success of the surgery and it showed.

That smile had always been infectious, and she returned it. For the first time since she'd arrived she thought they could have a good working relationship.

"Yes, they are, and you love it, don't you?" It was good to see, this glimpse of him at ease and in his element.

"Have to say I do." He placed his hands on his hips and looked overhead. "Looks like a nice night."

Emily nodded. "It is. I was thinking about going to the river to sit for a while." The James River gave peace to her soul. There were places she could go where she would be safe. No one would find her or accidentally run across her while on a walk, and she could let go.

"Really? You would still go down to the river even though it was our place?" Though he shouldn't have been surprised, some part of him was. The river used to be their spot, where they'd gone together to unwind, to splash in the shallows and toss off the stresses of the day. She still went there, and he hadn't been in three years. For some reason that surprised him. She'd been able to move ahead in areas he hadn't.

"Yeah. I still go. Not to our spot exactly, but nearby." She shrugged and looked away, watched her foot as she kicked a few pebbles off the sidewalk. "The water comforts me."

"I remember." The changing light reflected on her hair. What he'd known as a silky blond, down past her shoulders, was now a spiky mix of brown and red with platinum tips.

Unexpectedly, a lump settled in his gut at what she'd been through and how he'd been unable to help her, how he'd failed her. How she'd rejected him, and how he'd let her. She was an amazingly resilient woman and it was something that was very attractive in her. "You look good."

Startled blue eyes met his. In them he saw the woman that he'd once loved, but now the innocence had vanished, replaced by a strength and determination he'd never imagined she was capable of.

"You don't have to say stuff like that just because we're working together."

"I mean it. You look very good." That was probably something he shouldn't have admitted out loud, but she was a beautiful woman, short hair or long. "Different, but very good."

"Thank you." She took a step backward, away from him, almost shy again. "But I think I should go. Thanks for letting me know about the patient. I'm glad it was you working on her." She nodded, then turned.

"What are you driving these days? I can walk you to your car." He stepped up beside her, uncertain why he wasn't willing to let her walk away from him just yet. But he wanted to linger with her a few more minutes. Now that he'd gotten over the shock of her presence, he was more intrigued about why she was there.

"Small SUV, good for traveling but bad on fuel." She made that movement again, like she was tucking her hair behind an ear, but the hair wasn't there. That was what she used to do when she'd been nervous. "But I'm good. You don't have to walk me anywhere."

"I'd like to."

That made her stop and a smile lifted one corner of her mouth. "I take hapkido two nights a week, I can run a half-marathon and I have a big-ass can of pepper spray in my hand."

"Are you trying to tell me you can take care of yourself?" That thought lifted the corner of his mouth and eased some of the tightness in his chest.

"I am. I appreciate the offer, though." With the illumination from the streetlight he could see amusement sparkling in her eyes.

"Hapkido, eh? I don't even know what that is." That made him smile all the way. The thought of her in a martial-arts class, breaking boards with her forehead, just didn't jibe with what he knew of her. "No wonder you weren't afraid of that drunk."

"No need to be. I could have taken him down had there been a need." She leaned forward. "I would have protected you, too."

Now, that made him laugh full out. It was a good feeling. And having experienced the way she'd dropped him to his knees in the utility room, he believed her. "I have no doubt."

"Good night, Chase."

"Good night." He didn't say her name out loud. He'd vowed back then never to say her name again and watched as she disappeared into the night.

CHAPTER FIVE

BASKETBALL MADE HIM SWEAT. Handball made him sweat. Racquetball made him sweat, too, but nothing made him sweat the way last night's thoughts and erotic dreams of Emily had.

Dammit.

He didn't want to think of her, didn't want to remember, didn't want to want or hold or need or ache for her the way he used to. He'd moved on. He'd moved *on*. So had she. But last night it had all come back to him. All the pain, the pleasure and the bitterness. For just a moment there in the parking lot he'd been okay, been able to talk to her, but then he'd remembered. Really remembered. Against his will, against everything he'd vowed not to do, he'd remembered. And he'd ached for her.

Everything that had happened to her had been *his* fault. *His* responsibility. The changes, the tears, the rape, the attack, the sorrow. Everything. And there wasn't a damned thing he could do about it.

He couldn't change it, couldn't take it back, couldn't make it better, and it would never, *ever* go away. And he could never, ever forgive himself. Occasionally he could forget about it, but it never went away.

Rolling over on the bed, he looked out the window at the rising sun. At this time of the year life was in suspended animation. Fall and its crisp air hadn't hit yet, and the heat of the summer lingered on for a few more weeks, giving a false sense of pleasure that summer tranquility was going to last forever. Trees to the east glowed gold with the light behind them, the leaves taking on a gilt edge with each second that passed.

Unable to rest any longer, he dressed in running shorts, a T-shirt and trainers, then plugged in some music on his phone loud enough to quiet the voices in his head and took off out the front door.

At this time of the day morning joggers were a fair-weather lot. Some people he'd see on a regular basis, others only when the mood struck them and others sporadically. Today he didn't care. Foul in mood and in mind, he took off at a moderate pace, not wanting to injure himself but fast enough to challenge himself.

And he began to sweat. Again.

Someone slapped him on the arm, and he nearly stumbled. Slowing, he yanked the headset out, prepared to give someone a piece of his mind.

"What are you doing?" the man beside him asked.

"Dammit, what are *you* doing?" He'd forgotten. After the events of yesterday he was lucky he remembered his own name.

"You were supposed to wait for me." He took off, and Chase fell into place beside him.

"I forgot." Dammit.

"Forgot, hell. You never forget anything." Danny Hoover, firefighter, running and racquetball partner, and Emily's brother, jogged with him in the early-morning sun. You could have told me." He glared at Danny, unleashing the full brunt of his anger.

"Told you what?" Danny took the inner part of the path around a corner, and Chase moved into the outside position. Danny looked a little like Emily at times, but not so much that Chase felt he was looking at her when he saw Danny. Over the years he'd been able to compartmentalize things and just forget they were siblings.

"You know exactly what I mean. That she was coming back. You could have told me." Like he hadn't known.

Danny grinned and narrowly dodged a tree. "What, and take away the element of surprise? Besides, you said you were over her. It shouldn't have mattered, right?"

"I was. I am. It doesn't. But some warning would have helped." He *was* over her, wasn't he?

"Helped what?"

The man was a pea brain. Maybe he'd inhaled too many toxic fumes during house fires and they had begun to affect his brain. "The first time I saw her. It would have helped me prepare."

"Why would you need to be prepared? You said you were over her." Another turn on the path, a flock of ducks down by the pond looking for an early morning hand out.

"Because I…" Why had he wanted to know? Good question he really didn't want to answer.

"You want to be in control?" Danny provided the suggestion.

"No, I don't."

"Really? Isn't that why you're a surgeon? Couldn't be God and that was the next best thing?" He grinned.

Chase gave Danny a shove and nearly knocked him off the trail. "Where'd you hear that? That's not me, and you know it."

"Around the station. One of the guys is married to an OR nurse. Her opinion of surgeons in general, I think."

"I see. Which one?"

"No way! I'm not ratting her out. You'll just have to be on your best behavior in the OR from now on."

"Like that's gonna happen." He knew what most surgeons were like in the OR: giant toddlers with scalpels. He'd had his moments, for sure, but now that he was a little older, a little more experienced, his confidence in his skills had grown, and he didn't need to yell at the people around him in order to work with them. Others hadn't evolved as much.

"So, a leopard can't change its spots, right?"

"Don't change the subject. You're not off the hook for not telling me she was coming back." Hardly. Danny would be paying for that one for a long time.

"I know. But I couldn't decide which was worse, telling or not telling you, so I let the universe decide. If you two ran into each other then it was fate, meant to be. You're both grown-ups. You can deal, right?"

"Right." Chase jogged along in silence through the beauty of the low country, what was called the Tidewater, an area strongly influenced by the ocean tides. The area was filled with marshes and estuaries for waterfowl and major fishing grounds for the commercial industry. A place he'd called home his entire life. A place where something had been missing until yesterday.

"So how is she? I haven't seen her yet."

"Fine." He paused. "But she cut her hair." It had once been a source of pride to her, and he'd loved the way it had looked on her. Now she looked like a completely different person. Still beautiful, but very different.

"Oh, yeah, she did that a couple of years ago. Right after. Then." He cleared his throat. "What color is it now?"

"Brown and red and blonde."

"Ha. Used to be platinum, then orange for a while. Even dyed it black and gold for her favorite football team once." He shook his head and laughed. "She's a kick in the pants."

"Literally," he said, thinking of her new martial-arts

skills. "First day on the job yesterday and she took on some drunk without breaking a sweat."

"That's my sister. Doesn't take crap from anybody anymore."

"The guy was the husband of a patient. Beat his wife up pretty bad. Had to take her to emergency surgery, and then this drunk comes in, trying to give her a hard time."

"Emily wouldn't have taken too kindly to that."

"No. Especially not when the guy put his hand on her, or at least tried to." Chase still couldn't believe how deftly she'd handled that particular issue when he'd touched her in the utility room. His pride still stung that she'd gotten the drop on him.

Danny whistled as they rounded another turn. "I'd have paid money to see that."

"She was so fast." Chase barked out a quick laugh. "She was just cool as could be."

"Only on the outside."

"Huh?"

"She was cool on the outside, appeared to be calm. Inside, I'm sure there was a storm of rage boiling." They arrived to their usual turnaround spot and headed back the way they had come. "Been a problem for a couple of years, the rage, but she's learning to channel it."

"That's what she said later. She was meditating in the supply room. She never used to meditate. What's up with that?"

"She's learning new skills. Goes along with the martial arts. Calm mind, strong body. Nobody messes with you then."

"I see." Chase paused a moment, letting that sink in. He'd loved her once and wanted her to be whole again. "She did give me quite a warning when I touched her."

"Ouch! You still have a hand left? She could have killed

you without breaking a nail." He laughed. "I'm surprised she didn't."

"Still have both hands, but…I don't know why I touched her. Or tried to offer her some comfort." It had been stupid, even he knew that. They were over, history, and he'd had no business speaking to her in more than a professional way.

"Comfort? From you?" Danny gave a whistle. "Wow."

"Yeah, even from me. She didn't need it and didn't want it, so I left it at that."

"She's tougher than she used to be, that's for sure, but it saved her soul, know what I mean?" Danny gave a quick glance at Chase.

"I know what you mean. And I'm glad she's doing well. I hope she finds a place where she can be comfortable again, even if it's here."

"Really?" Danny stopped to laugh. Chase stopped, but didn't get the humor.

"What's so funny?"

"You are! You believe that crap you just told me? You hope she finds where she belongs, blah, blah, blah. *Really?* You're so full of it you can't see it for yourself."

"What are you talking about?" Chase tried to ignore the squiggle of something in his gut and it wasn't his breakfast. Maybe it was his intuition, or guilt, or maybe his conscience. In any case, it bothered him.

"You're not over her, never have been and never will be. So get over yourself, over your lies, and be a man. Go talk to her."

"I've talked to her. At work. Just yesterday." That was the absolute truth. He ignored the irritation rocking up his spine at the suggestion he was lying to himself.

"That's not what I mean, and you know it." Danny stopped laughing, his eyes now serious. "You owe it to her and yourself to see if there's anything left before you either of you can move on. It doesn't matter how much time has passed, it's not been over for either of you. It's time you settled it once and for all."

"Ha!" Pause. "Ha!" Pause. Emily faced herself in the mirror at her early-morning class at the martial-arts studio. This was the first place she'd taken a self-defense class and returning here felt like the homecoming she'd been waiting for. The people here had understood her needs at the time, after her attack, and had given her the skills she'd needed to defend herself and the privacy to work out her grief. She'd surrounded herself with women of courage and strength, and some little bit of those elements had seeped into her psyche every day. Every day she'd grown a little stronger, until she could stand on her own.

Then, it had been all she could do to live in the moment, let alone plan for an uncertain future. So she hadn't planned anything, other than going to the first class, then the second class, and the next after that.

"Hey, Emily, looking good." Approaching her was the dojo owner, Rose. Asian, small and petite, she looked as fragile as her name on the outside, but Emily had seen the woman take down men three times her size with hardly any effort. This was not a woman to mess with.

"Thanks." She rolled her shoulders and stayed focused on her stance. Focus was the key. If she let her brain loose, it just went wild.

"I wanted to ask you about teaching some classes for us."

Surprised, Emily lost her focus. "What? *Me?*"

"Yes, you." Rose took a stance beside Emily and mirrored her movements. "You're perfect, and uniquely qualified to teach self-defense classes for women." Rose referenced Emily's attack that had led to her quest in martial arts without bringing up the pain of it.

"I see." She moved into another position, held it, focused on her breathing.

"Do you? You're ready now." Reposition. Breathe.

"But I don't think that is my path." Reposition. Breathe. "I am a student of hapkido but not a master by any stretch of the imagination and certainly not qualified to teach."

Rose kept her gaze soft, looking at the floor far in front of them. "Are you going to make me say it?"

"Say what?" Had she missed something? Rose rarely spoke in metaphors or in the vague ways some masters did. She was just a regular woman with an interesting job where she got to hit people without being arrested.

"Seriously?" Rose broke her focus with a laugh, her eyes crinkling up at the edges, and she actually snorted. "You must be tired if you're missing this one."

"Oh, quit and just tell me." What? What had she missed? Was she seriously brain dead today?

"When the teacher is ready…" Rose rolled her hand in a circle, indicating Emily should finish the sentence.

"Oh, God…and the teacher will appear." She closed her eyes. "You have students already, don't you?"

"The first class is full, and we have a waiting list." Rose grinned at Emily in the mirror, and then returned to her pose. "Keep breathing. It will be okay. Remember, it's okay if all you do sometimes is breathe."

"I think I saw that one on social media somewhere." She narrowed her eyes at her friend in the mirror. She would have to reconsider the wiliness of her friend.

"It's been revamped for the current culture, but it's based on an old saying that doesn't translate the same way."

"So, when's the first class scheduled?" Emily gave a

mental sigh, knowing she couldn't let Rose or the students down. Just as her patients needed her nursing skills, these students might need her personal protection skills. If even one of them could protect themselves from an assault, it would be worth it.

"After we're through here we can look at the calendar and work it with your schedule. Just once a week."

"Oh, good." She relaxed a little. Maybe she could handle this. Maybe she could learn to be a teacher if it was just once a week.

"For now." Rose gave a Cheshire-cat smile.

"What?" Anxiety started to leak out her pores.

"No pressure."

"Really?" Emily raised one brow at that.

"Really. But with a waiting list…"

"You're *such* a bad liar. You have a plan already, don't you?" Why she was surprised, Emily didn't know, but she was.

"Of course. I'd love to have you become the key trainer for women's self-defense here." Rose clasped her hands together. "That would be just fabulous."

"You are out of your mind if you think I can do that." Really. "I have a career as a nurse."

"Yes. One that has served you well, and I'm not suggesting you give it up. I'm only suggesting you consider expanding your horizons, for lack of a better term, to help other women defend themselves in a way you could not."

Emily stood stone-faced. Her friend knew the whole story, the details of her assault as well as the aftermath and the agony she'd gone through. For her to make a suggestion was a serious thing, and one Emily was certain she hadn't considered lightly.

"You're really serious, not just yanking my chain?"

"I'm very serious. Women are determined to take care

of themselves, and they need someone to teach them how."
Rose also concealed her emotions from her expression.
"They need you, and I would be honored to help facilitate
their quest to find the right teacher."

Emily wiped the sweat from her forehead and faced
Rose directly. "I will have to meditate on this, but I am
honored and humbled you think I'm capable of this mission." It was a mission. She'd embarked on it when she'd
begun to heal and had never stopped. Maybe it was a
quest, as Rose had just said. Either way, she needed to
consider it from all angles before coming to an answer.

Placing her palms together, she bowed to Rose, who
returned the gesture.

"Meditate on it and let me know. You're ready." Rose
laid those dark, dark eyes, filled with knowledge of the
ancient ways, on Emily.

"I will let you know as soon as I can." She left the
studio with her heart a bit lighter and decided to stop by
the hospital to check on her patient from yesterday. That
should be a nice, short distraction, then she could go home,
shower, finish unpacking her stuff and make plans for the
next few days.

She knew how to work the system of being a travel
nurse. She'd been at it for years. Get moved into the apartment provided by the agency she worked for, unpack the
necessaries, get through orientation, work hard for three
months, and then move on to the next assignment. After
three years she had it down to a system that worked for
her.

Right now she was going to violate her own policy by
going to the hospital in her practice clothes, her *gi*, which
would give others too much information about her but
maybe it was time to expand her boundaries a little, let
her guard down just a bit.

She pulled into the parking lot of the hospital and parked in the employee lot, hoping she wouldn't run into Chase, that he'd be somewhere else, but as she put the car into Park she looked up and there he was, like he'd been waiting for her.

Was it her fate now to run into him at every moment?

CHAPTER SIX

TOO LATE TO back the SUV out, he'd seen her and nodded. He stood at the edge of the lot near the green space
where there were trees and a little brook where patients,
staff and family members could sit at the picnic tables
and visit or smoke.

Although the area was the designated distance from the
entrance for smoking, she could smell the ash a mile away.
Unable to leave gracefully and maintain her dignity, she
resigned herself to having to at least acknowledge Chase
as she went by him. Denying the kick in her pulse at the
sight of him just wasn't honest.

She clipped her badge to her *gi* and got out of the car.

"What are you doing out here?" she asked as she
approached him.

"Taking a smoke break."

She scoffed. "You don't smoke."

"No, but I'm entitled to the breaks, so I might as well
take them, right?"

What? Humor from the very serious Chase? "Uh...
right." She kept moving. "See you later."

"Not going to work in that getup, are you?"

That made her stop and face him. "Obviously not, and
I'd appreciate you not insulting me." Boundaries. Bound-

aries. Boundaries. Boundaries were everything now. In the past she'd have let it slide, but not now, and not with him.

"I didn't mean—"

"Yes, you did. You don't understand it, so you make fun of it. I get it." She'd dealt with that attitude since she'd started martial-arts training.

"I just didn't know what to call it." He moved closer and they fell into step together toward the hospital.

"There are any number of things you could have called it, aside from 'getup,' such as uniform, or outfit even, but you didn't."

"Sorry. Really. Sometimes I just don't know what to say to you." He huffed out an exasperated sigh. "I'm sorry."

"I understand, but you don't have to say something insulting or sarcastic just because you're uncomfortable around me. In fact, we don't have to see each other at all. Ever."

"How's that gonna happen? We'll be working together."

"We can be professional. Outside of that, I don't want to see you, Chase." Boundaries. Remember the boundaries. Very wide, very tall and very strong.

"Now, just wait a damned minute." He stopped, and moved as if he were going to grab her by the arm, then recalled her previous warning. "I work here. This place is my home. You're the outsider here, not me. I'm not going to walk around on eggshells just because you decided to come back here on a whim."

"A whim? This is my home, too, and I have a right to be here just as much as you do." She faced him, ire warming her blood. It felt good to let it out. To hold that anger in her hand and unleash it on him. "It was no whim that I needed to finally close out the chapter of you in my life."

"Then I suggest we be cordial, polite and professional."

She gave a slight toss of her head. "Fine."

"Good." *Uh-oh*. When women used to use the word *fine* things were anything but.

"I'm going to ask the charge nurse to assign me to patients who aren't yours."

"You can't do that."

"Watch me."

"You know it doesn't matter what the assignments are—when it hits the fan, you work with whoever is there. The patient is the important part of the scenario, not us."

"Then I'll ask to switch to nights."

"No. Don't do that, either. You can't work nights." In fact, she never could. Messed up her system and biorhythms too much.

"I'll deal with it." Pride lifted her chin and made her say things she didn't mean.

Chase sighed and some of the fizz went out of him. "No. Now, look. Don't do that." He ran a hand through his hair, frustrated beyond belief. "I don't want you to do that. It messes you up too much." He paused until she looked at him. "How about this? I just be professional, and you just be professional, and things will be just fine. You'll leave in three months, and we'll both move on with our lives."

She glanced away and crossed her arms over her chest. "I was thinking of staying here. Moving back home, I mean. Permanently." She shrugged. "It's my home, too."

"Really?" That surprised him. When she'd left it had been like she'd been shot out of a cannon. He'd never expected to see her again, let alone be working with her again. Now he knew the definition of the word *gobsmacked*. "Wow."

"Yes, wow." She took a breath and let it out slowly. "I'm taking the place for a test drive. See if the memories are too much for me. See if I can handle it again." After a sigh, she looked into his eyes. "I need to be home again. I miss it. I miss the people here. I need to put us to rest for good."

He paused a second, observing her expression, trying not to let any memories of her find their place inside him. "How's it going? Are the memories bad?"

"Not so far." She looked away. "Look, I just came to have a visit with Mrs. Billings, to see how she was doing."

"Well, as the surgeon, I can give you an update. I was going to see her again after my break, so now's good."

"Let's go." This reminded her of the old days, when they would round together on their mutual patients. It had given their work a structure that she'd liked and respected. Now this familiar pattern warmed her a little, and she sighed, feeling the irritation of a moment ago dissipate. It just wasn't important.

"Nice, eh?"

"What?" Had he read her mind?

"This getting back to our common ground, the things we knew, the way we used to do it?" He shrugged. "It's nice, right?"

"It is. Thank you."

They moved through the ER and to the elevators designated for staff. The elevator doors closed and the energy pouring off Emily was almost palpable in that confined space. "So, what kind of martial arts do you do, aside from hap…hap…?"

"Hapkido. Do you really want to know?" She turned curious eyes on him. Could this man be a genuine friend again? Could they put their past behind and be friendly? Only time would tell.

"Yes, I do." And he did. She was somewhat of a puzzle to him now. Not what he'd expected. And that intrigued him. Most people he could figure out in an instant, but this was a new Emily, and one who was puzzling him from all directions.

"I practice several. Started in hapkido, but moved on to try judo, karate and kung fu. There are benefits to each one, but the best for me right now is the hapkido."

"I hadn't heard of it, not until you mentioned it the other night."

"It's the best self-defense for women. It's Korean, but came to the States around 1980." She shrugged. "Probably why you've never heard of it. Relatively new."

"I'll have to look it up."

"You use some weapons, knives and swords, but the use of your body as a weapon is the most important. You might not always have a weapon but, no matter where you go, your body is always with you."

"True." He smiled at that.

The elevator stopped at the fifth floor, which housed all the critical-care units, including Trauma, Cardiac, Medical-Surgical and Pediatrics. Together they entered the medical-surgical ICU.

Emily paused when Chase stopped beside a patient room. She could see the patient inside whose bruised face from yesterday looked worse today. Pretty typical with the way hematomas evolved, they looked worse before they looked better. "Have you seen her this morning?"

"Yes. On early rounds."

Emily nodded for him to give report to her as a colleague.

"As you know, she's a forty-four-year-old female, entered the ER yesterday after being assaulted about the face and abdomen by her drunken husband."

"Yes."

"We opened her up and discovered, after your accurate assessment, that she indeed had a tear in her liver. By the time we got her to surgery she'd bled quite a lot. Once inside, we discovered that she appears to have some alcohol history of her own, but we managed to save her and the liver." He indicated the IV fluids hanging around the bed. "We have her on the DT protocol. Don't need her going into withdrawal while she's so critical."

"Certainly. I'd like—"

The cardiac alarm emitted its obnoxious call from Mrs. Billing's monitor. "She's crashing."

One look at the monitor and Emily saw the evidence of Chase's assessment. Lethal rhythm. They rushed into the room. There was no need to hit the code button as she was already in the ICU. Staff rushed to their side, alerted by the alarms.

"I'm sorry, ma'am. You'll have to leave." One of the nurses spoke to Emily. "No visitors now. I don't know how you got in here in the first place."

"I'm her—"

"Doesn't matter who you are, you need to leave." The older woman pointed to the door. "Now."

"Kim, she's with me. Emily was the ER nurse yesterday. She stays." Chase got all highbrow surgeon on the woman, leveling a stare at her. *O-o-o-h...* It seemed like he practiced that look, probably on the poor medical students, too. If things weren't so serious right now, she'd laugh.

"Oh."

"Get the crash cart," Emily said, also taking charge. "Open up the fluids till she gets here with the cart."

Emily did as instructed, programming the IV pump to infuse at a higher rate. As long as the kidneys were working, they could always get the extra fluid off the patient later.

Kim rolled the massive tool cart on wheels into the room and opened the top drawer. "Ready."

"Get the defibrillator charged and give her one hundred milligrams of Lidocaine." Emily took the medication Kim handed her and plugged it into the IV, pushed hard until all of the medication had been infused.

"Lido in."

"Charging. Two hundred." The whine of the machine signaled its readiness. Though she usually cringed at that sound, having Chase present decreased her anxiety.

Chase pulled the paddles from their cradle and pressed them against the patient's chest, one midsternum, one left side of the ribs. "Clear!" He squeezed the paddles, releasing the electricity into the patient's chest through the heart and hopefully disrupted the whacked-out electrical signal causing the chaos.

The monitor paused for a second, then beat, paused, beat again, then settled into a rhythm that was no longer deadly. "Check her pulse, make sure she has one," Emily said, and placed her fingers on the patient's swollen wrist, Chase listened with his stethoscope to her chest for a moment, then nodded.

"Good." He nodded and swung the stethoscope around his neck. "What's her Metoprolol dose going at now?"

Kim supplied the answer.

"Double it for the next four hours, get some blood gases, hematology and 'lights. Call me when they're back."

"Well, I had hoped she was going to be more stable than that." Emily spoke as they moved out of the patient room to the ICU doors.

"With the kind of injury she sustained, then surgery, then possible withdrawal, she'll probably be having more episodes, but I'm hopeful she'll survive."

"Yes, well, thanks, Doctor." Without meeting his gaze, she looked away.

Chase let out an irritated sigh. "I hate it when you call me that. It sounds so formal, so...old."

"Oh." She paused, uncertain how to proceed. "Then what should I call you?" *Your Royal Ass-wipe* just didn't have the right ring to it. But she'd come to make peace and continuing to annoy him wasn't in keeping with her quest. With a sigh, she let go of that, too.

"Chase, please. Just Chase."

"It's hard not to call you by your given name, but it adds familiarity I'm not sure I'm comfortable with right now." Not at all. But what had she expected? Obviously, she hadn't thought this plan through all the way.

"*Doctor* sounds a bit formal for us, don't you think?"

"Yes." Maybe she could get used to it. To saying his name without the emotional attachment to it she used to have. "I'll try."

"Are you going to head home now?"

"Yes. I have other things to get done today, then I work the next three days. Off for the weekend, though." Why had she told him about her schedule? Old habits, she supposed, the way they used to do. Easy enough to fall right back into them. She'd also fallen into step beside him, too close, so she moved further away from him as they returned to the elevators.

His eyes were serious as he looked down at her. It was always his eyes she could read and know what he'd been thinking. But now there was confusion and concern and something she didn't recognize, couldn't figure out, in his eyes. Curiosity?

"You don't have to be afraid of me, you know."

"I'm not afraid of you." Without meaning to, she raised her chin in defiance and felt the muscles in her arms tensing.

"You said that very quickly." There was that unknown

thing again in his eyes. Was it compassion or pain or grief? Or did he just feel sorry for her? She could tolerate a lot of things, but not that. Never that.

"What I'm doing is keeping an emotional distance from you—that's not the same thing." Really. She was not afraid of any man. Not any more. She could take care of herself very well now. She didn't need a man to protect her.

They remained silent as they left the way they had come, back through the ER to the parking lot. "You didn't have to walk out with me. I'm perfectly capable of taking care of myself."

"What, are you a lethal weapon now or something?" He indicated her uniform. "I don't know anyone in the martial arts, so I know nothing about it."

"And you're interested?" Seriously? Admitting that to her was a revelation. She didn't think he was really serious, so she wasn't going to waste any time with lengthy explanations. She owed no one an explanation about how she lived her life now. No one.

"Marginally." He shrugged. "More curious than interested."

"I see." Then it wasn't worth the explanation. "Then, yes, I'm a lethal weapon, if that makes it easier." Actually, she was. Now that she'd been asked to teach a women's self-defense class, she would be like Rose, the one students looked to for guidance. How could she be an expert when she didn't feel like one?

Her attacker—she refused to use his name or hear it in her brain—had been convicted and had received life in prison. He was gone, but there were others out there. There would always be situations where women would be vulnerable and needing to defend themselves. How could she turn down women who were looking for answers the same way she was?

"What were you thinking about just now?" He peered at her, shading his eyes with his hand. "You were seriously gone."

"What? Oh, nothing." She waved it away with her hand.

"Didn't look like nothing." His voice was calm and reminded her for a moment of days gone by, when they'd had good times, when they'd cared about each other's lives.

"Well, I've been asked to do something I'm not sure I am capable of doing or even if I want to." Didn't hurt to admit that, did it?

"What is it? Wait." He held up a hand to stop her from explaining. "You don't have to tell me, but the way I decide stuff like that is by asking myself whether it's helpful or harmful." He held up one finger and waited for her answer.

"Helpful." Definitely.

"Do you like doing it?"

"Yes." Absolutely.

"And would you learn anything from it?"

She sighed and let her shoulders drop, but her mind remained sharp and aware of her surroundings. That awareness never changed, would never change. "Yes." Undoubtedly.

"Then I'd say your decision is already made." He dropped his hand. "Well, gotta go save the world." He saluted her, turned away and returned through the ER doors.

She got into her car, started it up and drove away. Sticking to her training schedule kept her sane. Three times weekly she walked or ran five miles, twice weekly she practiced tai chi, hapkido was twice weekly, and she meditated every evening without fail. If work was stressful, she added an extra meditation.

Instead of taking medications for anxiety and stress,

she worked it out at the dojo on the mat. Her mind and body were in sync and it had taken commitment and practice to accomplish what she had.

Her phone rang, and she knew by the siren ringtone it was Danny. "What do you want, brother?" She smiled when she said it. She figured it was her job as the older sibling to give him a hard time.

"Hey, big sister. Whatcha doing today?"

"The usual workout schedule. Why? You need something?"

"The station is hosting a spaghetti-dinner fundraiser tonight and I thought you'd like to come by with an appetite and your donation to a worthy cause."

"Which is?"

"The Wishes And Hope Foundation for kids with cancer."

She knew the charity and it helped kids who were dying from cancer achieve one fantastic wish. "Okay, I'll come but I have a similar request for you." Turnaround was fair, right?

"Should I be afraid?"

"Only if you're allergic to a tux." He was, and she knew it.

"Uh-oh, what do you have in mind?" Hesitation sounded clearly in his voice.

"Fundraiser for the Rape Recovery Center." They had saved her ass after her assault and there was no way she could give them back what she had received, so this was a little help, something she could do for them.

"I see. Still helping out there?" The topic made him feel uncomfortable, but she wasn't bothered by his distress. Most men were uncomfortable with talk of rape, especially with the women in their lives. Good guys had a hard time imagining such violence against the women they loved.

"Yes, on occasion. This is a black-tie event, get dressed up for an evening of dinner, dancing and coughing up some money for a worthy cause. I'll cover the tickets, just say you'll go with me so I don't have to go by myself." She held her breath. He was notoriously difficult to pin down due to his work schedule as a firefighter, his need to test his manliness in adrenaline-surging sports, and general lack of organizational skills.

"Okay, what's the date?"

She gave it to him. It was three weeks away, and even he could get his life arranged to accommodate one night with his sister. "I fully expect you to pick me up and dance to every song I like."

He laughed into the phone, and her heart warmed. He was a nut, but he was her brother. "So you want the whole Cinderella package?"

"Yeah, but I don't want to turn into a pumpkin at midnight, though. Orange is not my color." Not with her hair.

"Gotcha. I will see to it that you have a lovely evening."

"And, for God's sake, clean out your car. If it was a building it would have been condemned."

"I will. See you tonight." The phone went dead, and she clicked off her hands-free device, suddenly looking forward to tonight at the fire station, saying hello to his work buddies. That meant she had to get her act together and get her workout done.

A good, hard run would help dislodge the images of Chase lingering in her mind and images from the past that began to surface. Some part of her wished she could just let those images of him hang out in her brain so she could visit with them a while. But there was no good purpose in hanging onto the past she'd worked so hard to forget.

There were times when images of Chase came to her, like the middle of the night, and she'd remember how

good they'd been together. Those nights she'd wake up
with tears on her face and an ache between her legs only
he had been able to assuage.

CHAPTER SEVEN

CHASE ARRIVED AT the fire station just in time to see Emily enter the building. He loved helping out his community by attending fundraisers, especially when there was food involved that he didn't have to cook, but, damn. He should have thought she'd be there. Danny was her brother first, before he was Chase's friend. The giant fire trucks were out front, all shined up for the public event. Cars filled the lot, lined the streets, and Chase had to walk a few blocks from where he'd parked the car.

Evening was approaching. Though still early October, the evenings were beginning to chill. Not enough for a jacket, but the damp air from the ocean so close by added a depth to the cold not found in dryer climates. He loved living this close to the water, surrounded by it, really, but there were times when the humidity complicated life.

The station was a madhouse. Kids ran around, screaming and carrying on, a continuous line from the hall itself to the large, inflatable castle jumpie-thing out front. Who knew what they were called, anyway? Kids didn't care. They just wanted to bounce around till they barfed. Good thing it had been set up *before* the spaghetti dinner.

Balloons, streamers, even a disco ball hung from the center of the room. No wonder they'd moved the trucks out. Needed room for all the chaos inside. The place sounded like a nightclub.

"Chase! There you are. Thought you might be held up at work or something." Danny approached, gave him a fist bump, then a one-armed bro hug. Several other firefighters shook his hand and offered him a hearty welcome.

"Made it." *Just in time to see your sister come in.*

"Grab a plate, eat all you want. Step up onto the scale now and after. We charge you per pound you eat."

"What?" He laughed. "Are you serious?"

"Kidding. It's a donation by the plate."

"Almost had me on that one." Danny was such a kidder, it was hard to know when to take him seriously.

Danny snorted and slapped his thigh. "You should see the women when I tell 'em that. They'd rather starve than get on the scale in front of a bunch of men."

Chase narrowed his eyes at Danny. "There's a reason you're not married, you know that, right?"

"You're right about that!" He pointed to his temple and nodded. "Too smart."

"That wasn't what I was going to say." Chase shook his head and got into line behind a family. There was the mom, dad and three girls who looked like they were all between the ages of eighteen months and six years old.

"Hi!" The middle girl waved at him, her bright blue eyes sparkling with an overabundance of personality. "I have two dogs." She held up three fingers on one hand.

"That's very nice." He grinned. Kids always spoke their minds and didn't have that pesky social filter ingrained in them yet.

"One is black, and one is brown." After that statement she nodded, as if mentally checking her colors.

"Is that right?" He couldn't help but smile at her enthusiasm.

"Yes." She bobbed her head and rose up and down on the balls of her feet. "One's a boy, and one's a girl."

"That's good."

"I know one's a boy because he has—"

"Sara!" The mother interrupted, a horrified expression on her pale face. "I think this man doesn't need the whole explanation."

"But—"

"No. He knows about boys and girls already." The mother gave Chase such a pleading look that he had to laugh. She mouthed "I'm so sorry" to him and crossed her eyes. Chase could see where Sara got her personality from.

The little fireball looked up at him, blue eyes questioning and curious, trying to determine the truth. "Do you?"

"Yes, I do." He nodded.

"Oh." She stuck out her lower lip and got back in line, obviously disappointed she couldn't share her vast knowledge with him.

"Sorry about that." Sara's father spoke to him and adjusted the toddler in his arms. "They say boys are a handful. Try three girls."

Chase laughed. "I completely agree." He looked at the little imp again. That was what Emily must have looked like as a child, all the wonder in her blue eyes, and gilt in her long hair that curled up at the ends. Then he sobered, realizing the youthful innocence that had attracted him to Emily in the first place was absent in her now. Curls had been replaced by short spiky locks, the gilt tarnished to a red-gold, and the innocence replaced by determination, anger and, somehow, courage of unfathomable depth. That saddened him to a degree he hadn't thought he was capable of feeling for her now.

After going through the line and dishing up a plateful of pasta, choosing a white sauce with clams from the

Chesapeake Bay, Chase nabbed a cup of some sort of red juice and a slice of fresh garlic bread. He sat down at a table a family was just vacating. It was the only one left in the house and, don't you know, the only one left behind was Emily.

"Don't say anything, just sit down and eat." She waved to the seat across from her. "We stragglers have to sit wherever there's a seat."

Soon they were surrounded by others and the chatter of children and families drowned out any pretense they could have made at small talk. Sara took a place beside Chase and sat with her feet folded beneath her in order to reach the table. The little chatterbox kept up more small talk than Chase had ever heard at one time.

"And that's how plants grow." She reached for her glass, but it slipped out of her little fingers.

The milk spilled, immediately followed by an ear-piercing scream, the pitch of which was enough to deafen people three counties over. Several people sprang back from the table, already accustomed to such mishaps at mealtimes with children. Unfortunately, Chase wasn't fast enough, and ended up with most of the cold milk in his lap.

Sara leaned closer and gave him an innocent look. "You got milk all over you, mister."

"I see that." He accepted the pile of napkins Emily handed to him. With her ninja reflexes, she'd managed to spring back from the table in time to miss the white flood.

"Looks like you're gonna need some clothes." Emily provided the succinct statement and smirked at the sight of his wet lap.

"I've got extra scrubs in the car." Trying to pluck the wet fabric away from his skin would only draw more attention to an area he'd rather avoid.

Just then the most obnoxious alarm rang out, lights

began to flash on the trucks outside and firefighters raced for their equipment.

"What's going on?" someone asked.

"They must have had a call." Although her brother loved his chosen profession, she still worried when he geared up to go out. She never knew if he would be coming home, but that was another area of control she'd had to give up. If Danny died in the performance of his duties as a firefighter, then he would die happy in service to his community.

Danny jogged over to them. "You guys should probably head to the hospital. There's been a ten-car pile-up on the freeway and, from the initial sound of it, it's bad."

Emily stood. "Right away. I'll go now."

"Come on. You can ride with me." Chase tossed down the wad of napkins. "It'll save time."

"Okay. Okay." She turned to Danny and hugged him. In his protective gear, he felt huge. "Be careful, please."

He grinned and winked at her, confident as usual. "Always, big sister, always."

Emily and Chase followed Danny out the door and quickly walked to Chase's car around the corner.

Fire trucks raced away in one direction, and they raced away in the opposite one.

"I wonder what happened." Emily chewed on her lower lip, a frown of concern marring the beauty of her face.

"It's always the same. Someone did something stupid, then someone else pays for it." Chase supplied the answer with disgust. He'd been at it too long to believe otherwise. It was the stupidity of humanity that people suffered from.

"I see."

Chase shot a quick glance at her. "I didn't mean anything by that." He clutched the steering-wheel tightly, feeling like he'd just stepped in it big time. He hadn't meant the remark to be in relation to what had happened to her in the past. He'd said he didn't want to walk on eggshells and apparently he wasn't. He couldn't monitor everything that came out of his mouth, could he? "Dammit."

"It's true." She turned to face the window, not really seeing the scenery. "It's the innocents who usually pay for the indiscretions of others, even something as simple as a lane change without looking."

Grim-faced, Chase focused on driving, getting them to the hospital without incident. There was nothing he could say, because it was all true.

They entered the ER together. "I'll go find some scrubs to change into." She looked down at her casual workout attire. "I want to at least look semiprofessional. I'll see you in a few."

"I'll have to change, too."

She disappeared down the hall. Chase headed toward the staff lounge, but was stopped by the charge nurse.

"Chase? What's going on? What are you guys doing here?" Liz asked, a puzzled expression on her face. "No one's hurt, are you?"

"No, we're fine. We were at the fire station when they got a call with a ten-car pileup, so we're anticipating you'll need us."

"Oh, wow. Absolutely right." Liz nodded, her expression changing to one of disbelief. "We don't have enough people on duty to cover that plus the usual mayhem." She grabbed the phone. "I'll start the disaster protocol. If I forget to tell you later, thanks for coming in."

"Sure. Gotta change, though." Chase entered the locker room and stepped inside.

Emily was there in a state of undress he'd not seen in three years.

"Get out." Emily grabbed her scrub shirt and covered

what she could of her body, but he'd seen her many times without clothing.

"No." Hell, no. Not when there was an imminent emergency breathing down their necks.

"Then turn your back." She stood still, staring at him until he nodded.

"Fine." He turned his back, then backed up toward the benches between the rows of lockers and began to undress.

"What are you doing?" She struggled to get the scrub top over her head. Punched her hand through the neck instead of the sleeve, reoriented it, and tried again.

"I'm changing for an emergency, the same as you." He whipped the milk-sodden shirt off and dropped his pants. Right there, in front of her, like he'd been doing it all the time!

"Well, stop it!" God. She didn't need to see him and all that muscle, those runner's legs. Not now. Not just when she'd thought she'd gotten them out of her mind.

"No. We're in a hurry. There's no time for modesty now. Besides, we've seen each other naked a million times."

"I don't care—it's not appropriate anymore." Seriously, not appropriate. Because it was making her mouth water and diverting her attention from the issue looming in front of them.

"Fine. I'll just pretend I didn't see anything." Like that was going to happen anytime soon. He'd certainly gotten an eyeful of her figure the second he'd entered the locker room. A man accustomed to making snap decisions based on quick assessments, he'd made one then. Beneath the loose scrubs and bulky martial arts uniform, Emily was a knockout, and he wasn't over her.

She'd toned her body to the point of very little body fat. The muscles in her calves and thighs were well defined, arms looked strong and toned and her abdomen looked like he could have bounced a quarter off it.

So that was why he turned his back, to hide the immediate and surging arousal his body had experienced when he'd seen her in just her bra and panties. Boxers weren't very helpful at hiding anything.

Pushing her feet into the loose scrubs, Emily tucked the shirt into the waistband and tied it tightly against her waist. She'd grabbed medium-sized scrubs and the legs were too long, so she put a foot up on the bench, rolled up the cuffs and secured each of them with a twist, then put her shoes back on. Her heart thrummed in her chest, and she was certain it wasn't just from the anticipation of the arriving traumas. Seeing Chase that way made her think of the many ways she'd seen his skin in the past, and she just didn't want to remember. She'd spent too many years trying to forget.

"I'll see you out there." Chase stuffed his clothing into a locker and went into the ER without looking back.

Having not been assigned a locker yet, Emily stowed her clothing in Chase's locker and closed the door, trying to ignore the whiff of male fragrance emanating from the unit, of the memories it evoked from deep in her mind. But it was the deodorant or aftershave that she'd always loved on him that locked into her mind and followed her out into the ER, suffocating her with memories of him.

CHAPTER EIGHT

"WHAT DO YOU need me to do?" Emily asked. Anticipation hummed through her as if she were going into an arena to spar with an opponent.

"Emily, you're with Chase in trauma room one. It should be set up, but double-check. You'll have the first patient through the doors so everyone else can wind up their patients and get them to the floors or discharged." Liz checked something off the paper on her clipboard and gave a brisk nod.

"Got it." Liz continued to act as unit commander, per the hospital protocol, giving out assignments and orders to those in her department. The usual assignments were on hold in this situation until they were certain of the toll of the disaster. Patients with minor issues were asked to go home, or seek care elsewhere. Most of them left, grumbling but understanding the serious nature of the request.

"Everyone get something to drink and a snack now. There's no telling when you'll have a break." Liz made an overhead page to all staff.

Emily entered the largest trauma room of the ER. There was enough equipment and space in there to handle just about any emergency, including the time they'd had to extricate a local farmer from a piece of equipment, a corn picker that had nearly taken the man's leg off. She opened up three bottles of IV fluids, spiked the tubings into them and hung them on poles suspended from the ceiling, ready to go.

Chase entered, his movements hurried and tense. "Suit me up."

Emily held out the blue paper gown for him, and he punched his arms through like a surgeon in an operating room. She moved behind him, tied the string behind his back and then held out the gloves for him.

"Have you heard what the first one is yet?"

"Yes. Gonna be ugly. Delivery truck with a load of fencing materials hit the brakes, the load shifted, and we're getting the passenger from the car behind it."

"Driver okay, then?" She gave him a hopeful look, but he shook his head and the look in his eyes said it all.

"No. Impaled through the windshield. Didn't have a chance."

"Oh. Do you know what kind of injury the passenger has?"

"We'll know in a few seconds but, guessing head, neck and chest injuries."

The doors burst open and the first patient arrived. The ambulance crew was high from the excitement of the rescue and pulling the person back from the edge of death.

"What do we have?" Chase asked, settling into his role.

"Fifty-year-old female passenger, sustained loss of consciousness. Bruising on forehead indicates she hit the dash. Lacerations widespread from glass, but none serious."

"Let's move her over." Emily directed the crew and six people prepared to shift the patient to the gurney. "One. Two. Three."

Smoothly and gently, the patient was moved onto the

hospital gurney and the crew pulled their cart out of the way.

"Vital signs are all over the place. Intubated in the field as a precaution because her oxygen level kept dropping. Not sure if she has a lung injury or not."

"Let's find out." Chase moved to the left side of the patient.

"Sorry, but we have to head back out there. It was worse than first reported. Lots of other crashes, trying to avoid the big one."

"Go. We've got it." Chase took his stethoscope and listened to the patient's lungs.

Emily hooked up the monitoring equipment then patted the patient's face. "Can you wake up? Cecilia? Can you open your eyes for me?"

The woman didn't move, her eyelids didn't flutter, and she didn't try to pull away when Emily pinched her earlobe, a minor test for response to painful stimuli. "Chase, she's not responding. At all." Emily pinched a fingernail, but the results were the same. Not good.

"Get Radiology on the phone. We need a scan of her head right away." He proceeded round the patient, continuing his examination, then stopped at the head of the bed and pried open her swollen eyelids.

Emily alerted the department of their need. "They'll be ready in ten minutes."

"Good. Lungs are good, belly's soft. I think the majority of what's going on is in her head," he muttered, almost to himself, as he listed her injuries.

"She's probably got a fractured femur, as well. The left is swelling up like a balloon."

"Dammit. If it's that fast, we've got trouble. Cut the clothing." Emily deftly sliced the patient's jeans from hem to hip with her trauma shears, scissors that could cut through sheet metal, then exposed the patient's leg for Chase to see.

"There." Emily gasped. A large shard of wood protruded from the woman's thigh. "Whoa. Didn't see that through the jeans." Emily whistled at the magnitude of the giant splinter.

"Being there is one thing—if it's punctured the femoral artery, that's another thing." He palpated the top of the thigh, trying to find the end of the irregularly shaped projectile. "I can feel it. We need to open it up before we do anything else."

"The head won't matter if she bleeds to death before we get to X-ray." Emily made the point and raised her brows at Chase.

"Right."

"What do you want to do first?"

"Get a cut-down tray. I can use that."

Heading to the cupboard, Emily pulled out the sterile tray and placed it on a bedside table. In seconds she had opened the wrappings, keeping everything sterile, handed Chase a pair of sterile gloves and poured half a bottle of Betadine cleanser into a cup on the tray.

Chase lifted his brows in amazement. "You go, girl!" He scrubbed the thigh near the splinter with the Betadine. "You could work in surgery. You're very efficient."

"Thanks, but I'll stick to ER. I'm too antsy to stand for long hours." A bit of warmth surged in her chest at his words. Chase wasn't one to offer compliments without cause. At least, he hadn't been in the past; no reason to think that would have changed about him. A person's core personality didn't change in three years. But it made her feel good to hear the words, reminding her of how well they used to work together. If only things hadn't fallen apart.

When Chase pressed the tip of the scalpel into the flesh beside the splinter and what looked like a river of blood flowed from the opening. "There's a gusher. Dammit."

"What do you need?" Not being an OR nurse, she couldn't anticipate the way they could, but she would try her darnedest to help Chase save this woman. Now she had to admit she'd missed him, missed this, missed working together when they'd been at their best. Tears pricked her eyes as sorrow turned in her chest. Unable to give in to the emotions right now, she forced them back and concentrated on the patient, on Chase's instructions.

"Put on sterile gloves. Put both retractors in and pull them in opposite directions so I can see where the little bastard is." There was such determination in his face she couldn't respond in any other way. Some part of her heart melted at this. This was what they did. They did it together, and they saved people. How could she ever have let go of that no matter what had happened to her? She'd been so stupid. So broken.

Emily complied and was able to do what he needed. Unaccustomed to the strain, her arms tired quickly, but due to her physical training she was able to focus and not lose her grip. "Got it?" Deep breath in, out very slowly. The tremors of her arms were transmitted to the instruments, but she hung on.

"There it is." He glanced up at Emily's face. "Hang on, baby, hang on." He continued to grumble and cuss at the bleeding artery as if it were a sentient organism bleeding just to annoy him. The click of clamps cut through the air as he identified the correct vessels and used the clamp to hold them in place. "Sutures." Without looking up, he held out his right hand.

Emily released one retractor and handed the materials to him with the needle clipped into another specialty clamp designed for sewing. "Sutures," she repeated.

"Suction."

"One second." She reached for the suction machine connected to the wall and pulled out the excess blood obscuring his vision.

"Perfect. You broke scrub with that hand." He said it without recrimination, just a fact to remind her.

"I know. Just the right, left is still sterile." She accepted his statement without rancor.

"Don't mix them up." He gave her a quick glance, then a nod of approval and a wink.

"I won't." Though they were in the midst of an intense situation, something inside her chest warmed at his gentle compliment of her skills when things could so easily have gone another direction. These were the kinds of moments that had bonded them, had knitted them together. Oh, how she had missed them! Now she began to tremble inside for an entirely different reason.

They worked together to finish tying off the artery. Moment by moment the chaos around them surged and crested as more and more patients were brought in, and the ER was filled to capacity and beyond. This patient was whisked away from the ER to Radiology, then brain surgery.

Chase and Emily washed their hands, changed gowns and gloves, and took the next patient. Hours and hours passed as they repeated the scenario several times. Though some patients had been diverted to other hospitals nearby, the worst came to them because they were the best.

"I feel like I'm in the TV show *M*A*S*H*." Emily shook her head in wonder and widened her eyes.

"Feel like you're working in a war zone?" Chase asked, and he gave a tired sigh. "Me, too."

"Yes. Just no one shooting at us."

"Yet."

"Don't you remember that one episode we watched?" Emily stood very stiffly, mimicking the character. "The one surgeon, and his famous quote: *I do one thing. I do it very well, and then I move on.* You could be him."

Chase huffed out a laugh despite himself, despite the exhaustion of the day and the critical patient lying between them. "It's true. I do have a tendency to be overly focused at times."

Emily laughed naturally for the first time since they'd been working together and it felt wonderful! It may have been the first time in years she'd felt this good. "And then, after we watched the *M*A*S*H* marathon, we…" She paused and the laughter slid away and the joy faded from her eyes as the rush of memories hit her. "Yes. Well. That was back then, wasn't it?"

Chase paused and met her gaze fully. He took a step toward her, his gaze burning into hers, urgency and questions swimming there. "Yes. And this is now." He cleared his throat. "Emily—"

"How are you two doing in here?" Liz asked as she charged into the room, looking frazzled and exhausted herself.

"I think we're ready to finish up with this patient, right, Chase?" Emily asked, looking away. He noticed a tremor of her hand as she reached for the surgical instruments on the tray table, and two of them clattered to the floor. She'd just exceeded every possible expectation with the surgical instruments, and now she had butter fingers? Something else was going on, but it would have to wait.

"Yes." He heaved out a sigh and rolled his shoulders to ease the stiffness there. That short moment when he had connected with Emily vanished. "How many more are out there?"

"We've cleared the decks. Eight damned hours later." She raised her arms in the air and did a victory dance around the room like a mixed-martial-arts fighter. "Wahoo! We did it. God, I'm tired."

"Eight hours? Are you serious?" Emily removed her protective gear. "I had no idea." She tossed the wadded-up gown at the trash can, but missed by a mile.

"This one is good to go, just needs a room with a view." Chase removed his gear and wadded it up, preparing to give it a toss across the room like a basketball player, but noticed a change in Emily, and he dropped the gown to hurry over beside her.

"You need to sit down." He hesitated to touch her, but she looked like she needed it.

"I'm fine. Legs are wobbly from standing so long." She attempted to take a few steps. "I'll shoosh it off in a mis-nus." She took those few steps, then her eyes went wide, and she reached for his arms. "Ch...Shase?"

He quickly wrapped his arms around her as she went down.

Liz dropped her clipboard and rushed to them. "What's wrong with her?"

"My guess is low blood sugar." His gut tightened as his brain went wild with all the crazy possibilities, but he wrangled them back. Keep it simple. Things like this were usually simple.

"I told everyone to eat something." Exasperated, Liz clucked her tongue.

"About ten seconds before we got our first patient, Liz. Neither of us had time to get anything." He hated snapping at her, but he was as worn out as everyone else, and his concern for Emily overrode his good sense.

"Let's get her to the lounge, we'll check her blood sugar and you two can get something to eat." Liz made the suggestion and held out her arm for Chase to lead the way.

"I'm slirpy fio."

Chase lifted her into his arms, some protective instinct tugging at his chest, wanting him to shield her as he should have done years ago. "Yes, you are slirpy fio. Now shut up."

He shouldered his way through the lounge door and set her down on the couch. Liz appeared seconds later with the blood-sugar monitor. "Let me see your hand."

Chase rattled around in the refrigerator and pulled out a jar of orange juice, poured some into a glass and held it to Emily's mouth. "Here. Chug it."

"Wait! Check the expiration date!" Liz held up her hand to stop him. "Some of that stuff's been in there for months. It could be rancid."

Instead of doing as instructed, Chase took a large drink of it. "It's fine." He returned the glass to her mouth. "Drink."

Emily took a few sips, then jumped when Liz pricked her finger for a drop of blood to check her blood sugar. "Ow."

"Really? That made you jump? Aren't you some hotshot kung fu expert?" Chase kept asking questions, trying to make sure she stayed awake until her blood sugar rose out of the danger zone. It kept his nerves under control and his hands from shaking.

"Hap-hapkido, An' that hurt." She frowned, and her lower lip stuck out. Before he leaned over and kissed that luscious lip, he pressed the glass against it again.

"More."

"Okay. Your sugar is forty." Liz provided the information with a downward turn to her mouth. "Too low, my friend."

"Oh." She drank the rest of the juice.

"You guys got this? I've got the rest of the crew to check on."

"We're good now. Go." Chase pulled a chair alongside the couch, needing to be a little closer physically to Emily, though she wasn't very happy about being touched by him. The close proximity appeased his need and didn't breach her boundaries.

"Got any protein in the fridge? Cheese or something? I'm going to need some when the juice is gone." She was no longer slurring her words, and she was able to hold the glass without trembling.

"Let me check." He rummaged around and found hard cheese, a jar of peanut butter and some bread. At the table he cut a chunk of cheese and handed it to her, then proceeded to slather the bread with peanut butter. Two slices. One for him, one for her.

"Great midnight snack."

"Actually, it's the after two a.m. snack." He sat again, the effects of exhaustion now hitting him. "Whew. I'm beat, too."

Emily looked at her watch with surprise showing on her face. "Seriously? Two a.m.?"

"Yep. If I didn't have to take you back to the fire station to get your car, I'd just crash in one of the on-call rooms." One of the few benefits of on-call: a readily available bed, no driving involved.

"I can call a cab. No big deal." She started to swing her feet over the edge of the couch.

"That's not what I meant, Em. Just meant…" He held out a hand to her, but hesitated. Then he looked into her eyes, wanting so much to connect with this woman, but he didn't seem to know how. Every time he faced her he faced his guilt, and it stopped him.

After a second's hesitation her eyes met his and the anger, the pain in them softened. Instead of being angry, instead of yelling at him or breaking his hand, she slowly stretched out her hand and laced her fingers with his.

"I know. It would be easier without me." The tone of her voice dropped with emotion he could feel pulsing off her. It matched the emotions churning inside him, and he looked down at her, at this petite woman who had been through hell. He wanted to reach out to her, to make it all go away, to somehow take them back in time to the place they used to be, to the people they used to be, but it was impossible.

"That's not what I meant, either." He dragged his hand through his hair and blew out a long sigh as she extricated her hand from his. "I'm just tired, too."

"We have to be back at seven. We'll only get a few hours of sleep." Now she was back to being professional and that moment of connection was gone. But she had reached out to him and that meant something, didn't it? She had let him touch her and had initiated the contact.

"Don't remind me. But there's more than one on-call room, there's a shower, we can eat here." He presented the option to her. It was what he would have done if left to his own devices. He didn't even have a house plant that required his attention so he didn't have to return to his place for days if necessary.

"I have a routine I do at night. I want my own things." She swung her feet to the floor and wobbled a bit when she stood. "Whoa."

"You're not fit to drive yet. Your blood sugar hasn't stabilized, so driving home isn't an option for you, either." There was going to be no argument about that.

"Well, I want to go home." She put one finger up. "Correction. I'm going home."

"Okay. You can go home, but only if I drive you."

"Then how will I get to work?" She took a few steps, testing out her muscles again, but grabbed on to the table. "Oh. Still dizzy. Dammit."

"I'll pick you up and take you to your car in the morning."

Liz burst through the door. "Okay. Schedule change for everyone. Since you can't realistically or legally show up here in five hours, we're sliding your shift back until eleven a.m."

"How are you covering the morning, then?" Emily asked, and folded her bread in half and took a bite, but leaned against the table for support.

"Nights will stay a little longer in the a.m., and then will come in a little later tomorrow night, then we'll be back on track with everything the next day."

"Good plan." Chase picked up his sandwich, folded it in half. "Let's get out of here before she changes her mind."

"Okay. I'm ready." Defeated, Emily followed him, too tired to argue any longer. Without a word she reached for Chase's elbow and tried to look nonchalant as she held onto him. Falling on her face would definitely have no dignity, so this was the lesser of two evils.

Immediately, Chase looked down at her, reminded once again of how they used to leave the hospital together after a long shift. She would lean on him, and then they'd sleep for hours tangled up together, drawing strength from each other as they'd slept.

They emerged from the ER into the dark and chilly fall night. Stars shone brilliantly overhead and a light breeze moved inland, bringing the scent of the ocean with it.

"Nice night." Chase led the way to his car.

"This is the kind of night I want to curl up with a fuzzy blanket and a hot cup of cocoa and just melt away."

"You used to do that, as I remember." The brunt of a memory kicked him in the gut as he got into the car. He paused for a second to take a deep breath. So much had happened to them. So much time had passed. So much pain had been left unresolved and it still haunted him daily, even though he tried to deny it.

"I indulged too often back then. Now it's a luxury." She reached for the seat belt and buckled it.

He started the car and pulled out onto the empty roadway, easing onto the street. "Where do you live?"

"Fisherman's Point apartment complex."

"I drive by there on the way to work every day."

"Then you know how to find it." She pressed her head against the cool glass window and closed her eyes, trusting him to get her home. When she felt Chase's hand rest on top of hers she didn't protest. It was an old gesture and one she drew some comfort from now. Besides, she didn't even have the energy to muster a defense against him had she really wanted to. All of it had been used on their patients, and she'd been drained dry. Her boundaries were at their lowest right now, and she cupped her thumb around his pinky, reaching out to him in a small way to offer him some comfort in return.

Shadows from the past haunted him as he pulled into the area she indicated. Without thinking, he'd reached out and placed his hand over hers. When he'd felt her thumb close around his finger, he had nearly been lost at that small gesture of connection. It gave him a small amount of hope that the connection they'd once shared hadn't been completely lost. He unbuckled his seat belt and turned off the engine. There was only one way to find out. Maybe right now wasn't the time, but he wanted to know.

"What are you doing?" she asked, her voice sleepy.

"I'm seeing you home. Safely." He opened the door and put one foot on the pavement. "No argument." Never, ever again would he leave her in an unsafe position.

"It's okay. I don't need you to do that." She opened her door and got out as well. Her movements were slower than usual, an obvious expression of the depth of her exhaustion.

"Too bad. I'm doing it." He exited the car and closed his door.

"Let me rephrase. I don't *want* you to do that. I can take care of myself." Though she stiffened, he didn't think she would be able to defend herself right now if she needed to. That protective instinct that had surfaced an hour ago kicked into overtime.

"I know, Emily. I'm satisfying my own needs right now, not yours." She couldn't even protect herself from herself right now, so he had to do it.

"Chase! Why are you doing this? I don't want you here."

"Because I need to." He made his way around the car to where she waited. "I *need* to, Em. Just let me."

"But—"

"You can't run away forever, Emily."

Brushing around him, she made her way to the door, and he hurried after her. He blocked her in the doorway as she was about to charge inside.

"I'm not running from anything, Chase Montgomery." He would not convince her otherwise right now, but he knew differently. She was running now just as surely as she had three years ago, but he wasn't about to let her run, not if he could help it. She'd come back here for a reason, and he was going to make her see the truth of it, of them, of what they might still recover, if it was even remotely possible. If it was, he wanted it. All of it.

"You've been running for three years, and you're still doing it."

"I've been building a new life. That's what I've been doing." She opened the door, and he shoved his way inside behind her, stiff-arming the door before she had a chance to slam it in his face.

"You've been building walls, not a life." Before she could shove him out the door he slammed it shut and followed her a few steps into the room, tempting fate as far as he could.

"I have not. Get out!" She spun, fire in her eyes like he'd never seen. His words had obviously triggered something in her, and he was going to see what it was right now. She snapped and crackled with electricity, and he was amazed as well as fascinated and aroused by the passion in her.

"Liar."

With a cry of outrage she pinned him against the wall before he knew what had happened. Though her height was much shorter than his, she had him. And he grinned. Then he laughed.

"What's so funny?" Her breathing came in short ragged gasps.

"You are. We are." Seriously. This was funny. Maybe he was exhausted, but this was damned funny to him. All of the tension from the day eased, though he was tied up like a pretzel.

"I am *not* funny." Her breath came in short gasps and she had apparently regained some of her strength. "Do I look funny to you?"

"I didn't mean it like that." He looked down at her mouth, breath coming quickly from between parted lips.

Lips he'd been wanting to explore since yesterday, since forever.

"You're saying that a lot lately." Her eyes narrowed as she watched him.

"Everything comes out wrong lately. You have me in an uproar on the inside." Inching his head closer, he focused on her luscious mouth. "Come closer," he whispered to her, the way he used to do before he kissed her.

She would remember that.

He couldn't forget it.

For just a second she dropped her gaze to his mouth, then returned it to his eyes. "Don't look at me like that."

"Like what?" Inching a millimeter closer, he was almost where he wanted to be.

"Like you want to kiss me." Her voice softened, and her gaze dropped to his mouth. She licked her lips, but didn't pull away. Her focus on him intensified, as if she struggled with herself to pull away.

"But I do, Em. I do. I've wanted to kiss you since the day began." What the hell? Why not? His voice dropped to a whisper and curious desire he had never expected to feel for her again surged through him. Before he changed his mind or she beat him up, he pressed his mouth against hers. It was the only thing he could move, as she had the rest of him tangled up in her tight grip.

The feel of her lips was something he'd never thought he'd experience again. She was soft and her lips clung to his as if she didn't want to let him go. God, he was in so much trouble. He should *not* have done that. But the fact was, he had. If he could get out of the clinch she had him in, he'd show her he didn't have to let go of her ever again.

CHAPTER NINE

EMILY COULDN'T BELIEVE he'd got to her. In this hold he shouldn't have been able to move, but he had. He'd kissed her.

He'd *kissed* her! Dammit, Chase Montgomery had kissed her!

And now she didn't want him to stop. Memories overwhelmed her, and she trembled from the onslaught of emotions.

Physically and emotionally he'd gotten to her, she'd have to admit that. His close proximity, his energy, the desire in his eyes had all gotten to her, and she'd dropped her guard. Gone in an instant.

Pushing away, she relaxed her hands, released him to do what he would because she could no longer fight him, or was it herself she was fighting? What he did was put those arms around her and draw her into his embrace, the embrace she'd fought to forget about, and now it was gone in a flash of heat and fire.

She *was* a liar, and he knew it.

He cupped her face with his hands, those long-fingered surgeon's hands. And he plundered her mouth, exploring with his tongue, coaxing hers forward. She didn't want to give herself to him, she wanted to hold still, to hold herself from him, but her defenses were weak from so much exposure to him in the past hours. And she couldn't do it. She wanted this connection with him too much. Maybe she would hate herself for it later, but right now stopping herself was out of the question.

Two days ago she never would have let him into her apartment, breaching her boundaries. Now? Now it seemed she'd changed her mind about him somehow, that she wanted him there, wanted him in her life again, contrasting sharply to her previous position. But was it really? Wasn't this exactly the reason she'd come back to Williamsburg? She'd had to find out if there was anything left between them and there was.

"I've missed you, Em." He choked out the same words that had been lodged in her throat. He'd been her friend, her lover, her partner, and she'd missed so much about him! He pushed her hair back from her face the way he'd used to when it had been longer.

"I've missed you, too." Pulling back, she looked at the face she had once loved and tears formed in her eyes. There were new lines of fatigue, probably from the crazy night they'd had. But the rest was the same. That little scar he'd gotten on his chin as a kid from falling out of a tree, the same crow's feet that fanned out from his eyes when he smiled and the lips, the mouth she'd loved exploring her body.

"Seems like you haven't changed much." Had he? Did she really know?

"No. Not much. But you've done a lot." He ran his hand over her spiky hair and watched it spring back into place. "This is really new."

"Yes. It's a new me." She dropped her gaze and retreated a little. "Not sure you'll like the new me. The old one is pretty much gone."

"So far, I'm admiring the new you a lot. You're stronger

than you've ever been physically, and that doesn't come without internal strength." He let his gaze run over her face, as if trying to reconcile the difference between the old Emily and the new.

He curved his hand around her ear, the way he'd done when her hair had been longer. Unexpected tears pricked her eyes at the bittersweet gesture. It was one she'd loved and it took her by surprise now. "I just wish…" His voice cracked, heavy with emotions too numerous to name.

"Chase…" With reluctance, she started to pull back. This wasn't what she'd expected tonight at all, and she wasn't prepared for it. Despite her months of getting ready for this assignment and coming up against Chase, in the moment she wasn't prepared.

"Give me just one more minute before I have to say goodbye again." The pleading in his eyes nearly undid her. The want, the need, the pain were all there and no longer hidden, the way they had been.

Uncertain, she raised her gaze to his and gasped aloud with the emotion struggling to break free, the pain in his face, the want, the need, the joy and the sorrow that filled her. She hadn't known the depth of his pain, but it was there now, exposed, bleak and raw.

"Chase…" The right words wouldn't come, and she leaned closer. She wanted to be close to him again, but in truth she didn't know if she could, if she was too broken to ever be that close to anyone again.

With a groan he reached for her, and she gratefully went into his arms. This kiss, this embrace nearly destroyed her. He reversed their positions so she was held against the wall by his body. He kissed her, devoured her as if he'd never get enough of her. Her arms went around his shoulders, and she held on like he was her lifeline, the way he'd used to be, and for a few moments she forgot.

Arousal shot hotly and fiercely through her and then the fear sliced through the heart of her, pushing everything else away.

She stiffened and instead of holding his shoulders pushed at them until he released her. "Stop, stop, stop. *Stop!*" She took a few steps away from him in the small kitchen, trembling from need and remembered fear. Sweat broke out all over her body. Her breath came in short, chirpy gasps, and she clutched the counter for support, embarrassed that panic had hit her at such an inopportune moment. She'd never tried to make love with anyone except Chase since the attack, so her reaction shouldn't have surprised her. After all the counseling she'd had for PTSD, and all the martial-arts studies, she'd hoped she'd gotten further along in her recovery, but here she was. Not.

"I'm sorry. I should have let you go, but I didn't want to." He watched as she prowled back and forth from the counter to the wall and back again, her thoughts inward, and he didn't even know if she heard him. "Emily?"

"What?" She looked up at him, eyes wild, and he was certain she was having a panic attack. He'd seen her like this before and it had been right before their breakup. The first time, the only time they'd tried to make love after the assault it had ended badly, ended with a rift so wide they hadn't recovered from it. Neither of them had been prepared or able to cope.

"It's me. Look at me. Talk to me." The pain of watching her was like someone had taken an ice pick and stuck it in his gut.

"I can't. You need to go now." Her hands shook as she took hold of the counter again.

"I'm not going anywhere." Never again would he leave her in a fragile state, no matter what the reason. He was a better man than he'd been three years ago. He needed her to know that.

"Go." She pointed to the door, but her eyes were still wild, agitated, filled with demons from the past.

"No. I'm not leaving you the way I did before." The guilt of that had weighed on him for years. "I won't ever leave you again like that."

"I don't need you, Chase."

"But I need you, Emily." He took a few more steps away from her and moved into the living area, hoping she would follow. "Come sit down for a few minutes."

Numb, she followed him, trying to figure out how she was going to get him out of her apartment, to take back her peace. "I need to do my relaxation exercises before I can go to sleep."

"Then do them."

"Not with you here, watching me."

"I don't know how to do anything remotely relaxing, so why don't you give me a lesson? I need to learn something to help me sleep that doesn't consist of a medication or alcohol."

"Seriously?" Doubt covered her expression, and he deserved it. He hadn't been very supportive of her self-care practices.

"Seriously." He sat down on the floor and tried to cross his legs the way he'd seen her do, but he couldn't.

"You don't have to do this." She plunked down beside him and crossed her legs easily. Show-off. "It's completely unnecessary."

"I want to, but my legs won't go the right way." He shrugged. "Besides, it will be a distraction for you to have a terrible student. Can't get any worse than me, right?"

"Right. You need to stretch more, or you'll be a stiff old man who can't tie his shoelaces. For now, just straighten them out in front of you." She let out a slow sigh, then took in a breath.

He did as she said and there was an immediate release of the tension in his body. "That's better. Now what?"

She gave additional instructions for his positioning, knowing what he was doing, distracting her from the panic. Since it was helping a little, and there was some ease of tension between her shoulders, she continued. "Now, close your eyes and listen to the sound of my voice." She took a cleansing breath in and let it out slowly.

"Okay. I'm listening."

"Now, close your *mouth* and listen to the sound of my voice."

Amused, he cracked an eyelid at her, but she was concentrating, her eyes closed. He tried to mimic her as he took in deep breaths, held them for a count of three and then released to a count of five.

As she led him through the exercise, his body began to relax. The tension in his shoulders loosened and the humming in his groin began to ease. Amazing that just breathing could accomplish so much.

Moments later he began to nod off, his body relaxed, and he realized she'd stopped talking. Opening his eyes slowly, he wasn't sure what to expect. But seeing Emily's gorgeous eyes watching him made him freeze.

The moment, the connection, the electricity between them was nearly palpable. He wanted to reach out to her, to touch her, but he was afraid if he moved the moment would vanish and so would she.

"I'm going to bed now. There's a blanket on the back of the couch you can use." This time, her voice was calm, the wildness was gone from her eyes and the relaxation had obviously done its job.

Graceful and controlled in her movements, she rose

from her position on the floor beside him. Before she disappeared and the moment was gone forever, he clasped her wrist gently in his hand. He wanted to drag her down onto the couch with him and tear their clothing off, make love with her until they were both spent and exhausted. But he didn't. It wasn't what she needed.

"Thank you," he whispered.

"For what?" She didn't pull away or move but stood there for a moment, seeming transfixed.

"For helping me learn something new, opening my eyes to things I never would have otherwise considered. I didn't expected anything like this when I got up this morning."

A small smile tilted up one corner of her mouth. "Neither did I." She eased away from him, and he released her wrist, but the warm, smooth feel of her skin sliding against his lingered. "I'll wake you when it's time to go in."

"Okay. Good night."

"Good night." Emily turned to go and wished for just a moment that she could invite him into her bed, that things were different between them and they could love again.

Dropping her clothing by the bathroom door, she paused as a surge of unexpected energy pulsed within her. The kind she hadn't experienced in years, not since before the attack and subsequent rape that had drained her of feminine energy, feminine power, and her sexuality. This close proximity to Chase was having quite an effect on her nerves.

Stepping into the shower, she turned her face to the spray, wanting to drown out thoughts of Chase on her couch, Chase in her apartment, Chase in her arms. Chase in her bed.

"Emily." Chase spoke, his voice raw and husky from the doorway.

"What are you doing in here?" The shower curtain

offered little protection, but she pulled it against her, anyway.

"I heard the shower." A deep bruised look haunted his face, as if he was remembering their past together, too. Dark circles deepened his eyes.

"And, what, you thought you'd join me?" Damn. She shouldn't have said the words out loud. Now they were out there to become real.

"I could use one." Chase approached. He still wore his scrubs, still had that bruised, exhausted look about him, and her heart broke. The casement that had protected her for three years fractured.

She'd never felt more vulnerable.

He'd never been more wanting.

With her gaze glued to him, she drew back the curtain, silently inviting him inside the cocoon of heat and water with her. This day was a time out of time, a little bubble of protection where they could forget about the past and just live together in the moment.

In seconds he'd stripped and entered the shower with her, keeping his eyes on hers. Doing the dance to adjust positions in the narrow space, they pressed against each other, sliding slick bodies against each other until Chase had his back against the spray. Tilting his head back, he immersed himself fully under the water and rubbed his hands over his face and groaned. "Oh, God, this feels good."

When he leaned back, Emily used the moment to take a good look at his body, at what she'd been missing for three years. Swallowing became difficult and her heart thundered in her chest, roaring in her ears over the sound of the shower. Remembering to breathe also seemed a foreign concept at the moment.

He'd dropped some weight, was now made of lean muscle and sinew, and looked like the runner he was. Long and lanky, arms and legs were finely muscled. His chest sported a light sprinkling of hair across his pecs and a finely muscled abdomen tapering downward.

Without removing his gaze from hers, the only thing he moved was his hands, to reach for the body scrubber and body wash. He poured a generous amount onto the scrubber and squished it up so it made suds, the way she liked. He'd said he remembered everything and seemed that was so right now.

"Turn around," he said, and she complied. Maybe if she didn't see him, she'd be okay. Maybe if… The scrubber hit her back she closed her eyes at the stimulating touch. Chase applied it to her skin in circular strokes, beginning at her shoulders then moving downward.

She placed the palms of her hands on the wall in front of her, needing the support. He touched her nowhere else, just with the scrubber. Beginning at her wrists, he stroked her skin, stimulating, teasing and torturing her body and her mind.

She hadn't surrendered control like this in forever and it was overwhelming, standing still as the scrubber moved over her neck, and she tilted her head back to give him greater access. The heat from the water and his body created a steam that nearly choked her. Or was it the heat of attraction that had never left her?

He was tall enough to reach over her shoulder and apply the scrubber to her chest, her breasts, teasing around each nipple until they were tender, stimulated peaks, aching for more. Moving his hand beneath her arm, he moved the scrubber across her upper abdomen, then her lower abdomen, then between her legs.

"Lean back," he said. "Let me take your weight. You can trust me." He stroked the hair back from her face and with a little pressure on her forehead eased her head back against his left shoulder and stayed that way until she released the tension in her muscles and let her weight fall against him. "Trust me, Em. I won't drop you, ever again." The feel of his erection against her backside aroused her more than she thought possible. He was hard and sleek and ready for her.

It was so foreign at first, to lean back against him, to let him hold her against his body, to let him stroke her. Turning her head slightly, she leaned her face toward his and he kissed her.

It wasn't the out-of-control passion they'd had in the past. This was a kiss of deep reverence, of passion and honor, and of a man seeking forgiveness.

She parted her lips and allowed him in, allowed him to take her where she'd longed to go since the first time she'd seen him again. Had it really been just days ago?

Three years away from him and it seemed like just yesterday she'd been in his arms.

Groaning, she turned to face him, clutched his shoulders and plastered her body against his. His arms went around her waist and pressed her harder against him, his hips jutting forward into hers, his erection hard and demanding against her abdomen.

Kisses ranged everywhere, and he scooped up one of her nipples in his mouth, teasing it without mercy. The rasp of his light beard stimulated her sensitive tissue. She clutched his head to her chest, spreading her kisses wherever she could reach.

Then her hand moved between them, but he stopped her, his grip like a vice on her arm. "This isn't about me tonight, Em. I don't want you to…be uncomfortable."

"Then just hold me for a little while longer."

"I will." He pressed a kiss to her head and let the water

wash over them, cleansing their bodies and maybe a little of their souls.

After long moments passed and she relaxed, the stress of the day faded away. "Are you getting cold?" Her head fitted snug and perfectly beneath his chin. He'd forgotten that.

He'd missed that.

"What?"

"The water's getting cold."

"I hadn't noticed." Seriously, hadn't noticed.

They got out of the shower, dried each other off in between kisses and sighs. Emily was wrapped in her bulky robe and she hesitated at the door.

"What's wrong?"

"I don't know." She looked like a sprite with her hair all spiky and wet, her eyes huge and dark, her mouth swollen from his kisses.

He approached, wrapped only in the towel. "Why don't you tell me what you do know?"

"It's so hard to put into words." She stood there swallowed up by the robe, arms hugging her middle.

"It's wonderful and awful at the same time, isn't it?" He shared the thoughts swirling like mad inside him.

Tears flashed in her eyes, and her chin trembled. "Yes."

"Why don't we go to bed, and you can tell me.'

"It's probably five a.m. by now. I don't want to keep you up any later than necessary."

Indeed, his body was telling him things he didn't want to know about, like it was going on twenty-four hours since he'd been horizontal. "I don't care what time it is. If you want to talk, I'll listen."

CHAPTER TEN

"WILL YOU HOLD me awhile? Just hold me. I won't ask you for more."

"Yes." He didn't trust his voice to say any more than that. He was exhausted and choked with emotions he couldn't name.

She led him to the bedroom, dragged the covers back and they got in. She'd always liked to be on her left side with him cuddling her from behind. That was the position they gravitated into now, and Chase felt like the past three years had fallen away from him in an instant.

But now she was tense.

"Do you want to talk?" Although he whispered in the dark, it sounded very loud.

"I...I... The words won't come." Her voice was small and soft, evoking the protective side of him from the place it had hidden, licking its wounds, for three years.

"Relax. Sleep. Let me hold you. I'll keep you safe." The soft breathing and the gentle rise and fall of her chest soothed him. Again, she fitted him perfectly, fitted in a way no other woman ever had.

There was no reason for her to fear him, but she didn't know that. It was up to him to tell her, show her, prove to her that she could trust him again. She'd deny she was afraid of anything, but deep down he knew he was right.

Unable to keep his mind awake any longer, he pressed a kiss to the back of her head and allowed sleep to overtake him, more content than he'd felt in a very long time.

Hours later he awoke to the scent of coffee brewing and the sun bright in the window. Emily was gone, her place beside him cold. Easing from his place, he grabbed the towel from the floor and wrapped it around his waist.

He paused in the doorway when he noticed Emily performing a series of slow movements, a small rubber ball in her hands. She was graceful and elegant as she moved the ball around, then she stopped when she saw him.

And smiled.

"I'm sorry. I didn't want to interrupt you."

"No problem." She released the position she was in and placed the ball on the couch. "I was just about through, anyway."

"I smell coffee. What time is it?"

"Noon." She padded on bare feet to the kitchen.

"*Noon?* Aren't we supposed to be at work, like, an hour ago?"

She was obviously unconcerned, and that wasn't like her. She was never late for anything.

"I got a text that staffing had changed once again. Since we were the last to go home we get the day off. They found some staff to cover." She nodded to his phone, which lay on the counter. "Check your phone. You probably got the same text."

"Wow." He checked the phone. "I haven't had a day off in like a billion years." Seriously.

"Well, I've got coffee going, but don't have much besides a few essentials."

"Whatever you've got is fine, or I can just have coffee and go." But as he looked at her, he didn't want to go. He didn't know what he wanted, what he needed, or what she needed, either. "Or I can stay."

"Actually, I'll need you to either drive me to the studio or take me to my car."

"The studio?"

"The Rose Lee Martial Arts Studio. The dojo where I practice." She shrugged and reached for two mugs, filled them with coffee and opened the fridge for the milk. "Since I have the time today I thought I'd go over there and mess around."

"Since I've got no other plans, how about I go with you?" Watching her face, he looked for signs of tension but found none. Joy and happiness weren't there, either. More resignation.

"I'm not sure you'd like it there. Very martial-artsy."

"After seeing you in action a couple of times, I have a new admiration for the art and would like to watch you work."

She considered him a moment, her eyes narrowed, and she tilted her head to one side. For some reason, he felt much like a mouse being stalked by a cat. "Do you have scrubs in the car?"

"Yes. I always carry extra."

"Just so you know, at Rose's no one is an observer. If you're there, you're there to participate. If you're not intimidated by that, you can come—otherwise you can take me to my car, and I'll go by myself." She just left the words to hang in the air a moment for his consideration.

"That has the smell of a challenge in it." He was not above a good challenge, but this one could have unforeseen consequences. Things could go either way. He had to decide quickly if he could deal with it.

"Call it what you like, but those are the rules."

"I'm up for it." He sipped the brew, hot, strong and bold,

just the way he liked it. And a good description of what
Emily had become. He liked that, too.

Within the hour they arrived at the studio, Emily in her
gi and Chase in his scrubs. They removed their shoes at
the door and entered the practice room. During the day
few people were there, but at night the place was packed.

At the moment Emily was glad of the space. She'd
hardly had a chance to catch her breath in the last few
days, and now here she was, about to take Chase to the
mat, literally.

"Chase, this is Rose, owner of the studio and my
teacher, my *sensei*. You may address her as Rose or *sensei*." Emily gave a slight bow from the hips, as did Rose.
Chase followed their lead.

"He is a tall one," Rose said, her eyes scrunching up
at the corners. She was just over five feet tall, so Emily
had her by a few inches, and Chase towered over both of
them by quite a bit. "I'm not sure you can teach him. He
might need someone taller." She looked up at Chase as if
he were a tree.

"I am happy to have Emily teach me a few things. She
nearly took on a man larger than her at the hospital the
other day and height didn't seem to matter."

"I see." Rose gave Emily a look with raised brows but
a serious face. "So you have already defended Chase at
the hospital?"

"Yes, well, no, not really. The man was intoxicated
and upset. No one got injured and Security escorted him
away." She explained the situation in dry terms, giving
only the facts. "But I would have, had the need arisen.
As it was, Chase defended me, or perhaps we defended
each other." As she said the words she looked at Chase,
and he nodded.

"Have you considered what we previously discussed?" Rose asked.

It was not a question without consequences, and Emily had considered it from all angles.

"Yes, *sensei*, I have. I will teach one class for you and see how that goes."

"What class is that?" Chase asked, suddenly very interested in their conversation.

"Self-defense for women. There is a need for good teachers at my studio. Emily has the soul of a warrior and the heart of a teacher. I believe she will be the best person to teach this class." There was no false flattery in her words, just simple facts.

Emily bowed, her face flushed and pink. "Thank you, *sensei* Rose." She clasped her hands together in front of her heart and gave a slight bow. "Thank you."

"Please, proceed with what you were going to do, and we'll talk schedules later." Rose returned to the office, leaving Emily and Chase alone.

"What were you going to do if you were by yourself?" Chase asked, curious about the little warrior in front of him that he was beginning to get to know.

"I was going to do some sword work, but I can do that another time."

"Sword work?" Now, that was impressive. She was very serious about this. He'd never have guessed.

"Yes, it utilizes different muscles than you would in running or sparring. But now I think we'll start with basics." She looked him up and down, deciding on what to do.

"What would you teach in your class?"

"Basic self-defense."

"Show me something."

She thought for a second with her lips pursed. "Okay.

Reach out to me like the guy did in the ER. Like you're going to grab my shoulder."

Hesitating a second, he reached out slowly, not wanting to hurt her.

"Come on. Do it like you mean it. Charge me if you have to."

"I don't want to hurt you." This was so weird. Even in play it felt uncomfortable.

She snorted. "You can't. Now do it!"

With a toss of his head he did what she'd asked. Before he knew what was going on he was on the floor, looking up at the ceiling.

"Oh, Chase! Are you okay?" Emily knelt beside him, serious concern in her eyes. "I'm sorry!"

"What happened?" He blinked a few times, but nothing seemed broken, and he still had his testicles, though they were cringing against his bottom. All good.

"Well, I think I went a little overboard." She bit her lower lip, hesitating but not afraid.

He struggled to a sitting position and let her help him up. "I reached out like you said…"

"I should have just pinned your arm behind you. But instinct kicked in, and I swept your feet out from under you, too. Jeez, I'm sorry." Trembling, she pressed a hand to her forehead.

Rose approached, her face the picture of serenity. "Don't worry. Even teachers make mistakes. Better to make one now with him than later in your class."

"But what if I hurt someone? Unintentionally." That was her biggest fear about teaching women who had no skills. What if she made them worse?

"You could. You probably will at some point. But it will be a lesson they need." Rose looked up at Chase, considering, but kept her thoughts to herself. "Carry on. You'll be fine." She turned to Emily. "You're a good teacher."

"Thank you, *sensei*." Emily bowed slightly as Rose left the room again.

"Okay. Let's try it again. I'll grab your shoulder like this." With his left hand, he reached for her right shoulder.

"Then I push your arm away and wrap my hand all the way around your arm with my right, push your shoulder up to the point of pain and use my left hand to control your head movement away from me." She held him that way for a second. "Ha! That's it."

"You really do have me in a grip there." There was no wiggle room at all.

"Now try to get free."

He struggled to move and extricate himself, but he couldn't, not without causing himself pain. "You're hurting me. No matter which way I try to move, it's painful."

"I'm not hurting you. I'm simply holding you still. When you move *you* are causing yourself pain. Eventually an assailant will learn to hold still because he is causing himself pain. Even if it's a woman who is holding him." She released him, and he rolled his shoulder around, easing the joint, and the pain ceased.

"Wow. That's really impressive." Eyes wide, he looked at her anew. "You're really amazing. Do you know that? I mean *really* know it? How powerful you are?" He was just beginning to understand it himself.

She stared at him, met his gaze straight on. "I wouldn't have had to become any of this if I hadn't been raped."

That statement punched him in the gut like he'd been assaulted himself. His chest tightened and it felt like a vise clamped around his throat. He swallowed, hard, emotions strangling him. "I'm sorry."

"It's not your fault a serial rapist broke into my apartment, beat me up, raped me and tried to kill me."

He swallowed. There it was. The statement of what had happened. What had nearly killed her, but had made her stronger, had broken them apart and nearly destroyed him. "I don't know what to say. In the past everything I said was wrong." Why should it be different now?

"There's not a lot to say." She sighed and the energy seemed to puddle out of her. "I think I'm done for today."

"Is it because of what I said?" Again.

"No." She dropped her gaze away from him and withdrew into herself. She began to walk toward the door, and he followed, his heart heavier than it had been in a long, long time. There was nothing he could say to change the past, nothing he could say to change the present either. Time healed some wounds, but others stayed raw forever.

They found their shoes and headed to the parking lot. "Do you want me to take you to get your car now?"

"Yes. I think that's best." She sat in the passenger seat, looking out the window, as Chase started the car. By now the sun had passed its zenith and was on the long, slow decline down to the horizon.

The radio played low in the background, but it was the only thing that broke the silence in the vehicle. Emily had withdrawn, and Chase didn't know how to bring her out. He didn't know if she would ever recover from her assault. Was it reasonable to expect that she would? He just didn't know.

"He's gone for good now." She spoke to him but still looked out the window.

"Who?"

"Bernard Twist. The rapist." She'd come to think of him as Bernard Twisted. The things he'd done to women had been gut-wrenchingly awful.

Without answering, he negotiated a turn and then another. "I know. I followed the trial."

"He's such a sick bastard, but I have no sympathy for
him. None whatsoever."

"I wanted to kill him." He pulled up near the side of
the firehouse and parked, but kept his hands on the steering-wheel. The tremors inside him were visible, and he
clutched the steering wheel harder. "If I'd found him before the police, I think I would have."

She turned, surprise on her face. "Really? You wouldn't
just have let the police handle it?"

He shook his head in an anger, a hatred so deep even
the memory of it scorched him. He blew out a breath. "I
don't think I'd have been able to control myself."

Emily stared at him, seeming to come to a decision.
A small smile lifted one corner of her mouth. She leaned
toward him and placed her hand behind his neck, pulling
him forward, and pressed her forehead against his.

"I'm glad you didn't, but thank you for thinking of it."

"You're welcome." That was kind of funny, being
thanked for murderous thoughts.

"Sometimes I forget I wasn't the only one who was
raped. You were assaulted in a different way, and I'm
sorry for that, Chase." She stayed that way, not moving,
just breathing.

Then he realized she was saying goodbye to him without words. "Wait a minute."

"I'm going to go now, and I'll see you at work."

"I don't want that." He pulled back, but took her wrist
in his hand and held her hand to his face. "I mean, I don't
want to just see you at work."

"A relationship between us won't work. I thought perhaps there might be a chance for us, but I was wrong. I
needed to come here to see it for myself. You've seen

how messed up I still am, probably will be the rest of my life. I want to focus on my work at the hospital, at the studio, and with the new class I'm going to teach." She gave a watery smile, her lips pressed together for a moment, trying to control her emotions. "That's enough for me. It has to be. If I want too much, I'll be disappointed the rest of my life."

"No, it's not. It never was. And it's not enough for me." Anger began to boil inside him. Being ripped apart at the seams twice wasn't acceptable. Somehow he had to change this. Somehow he had to get through to her. Somehow he had to make her see.

"The old Emily is gone. I still have the same name, but the rest of me has changed. You need to face that, Chase, the way I did. I'm not the woman you once knew, you once loved." She pulled the handle on the door and eased out of the car.

Danny was trotting across the parking lot, waving. Any moment Chase would have had to talk to her about their situation now was gone, and he might never get another chance. The walls around her he'd breached for a little while were now as high and strong as ever. Maybe he was chasing the wrong Emily. Maybe he was chasing a ghost that no longer existed, and she was right. Maybe the Emily he'd loved was gone, and he needed to move on for good. Or maybe he needed to chase *this* Emily and see where she led him.

He wasn't giving up.

He watched through the window as Danny hugged his sister and met Chase's look over her head. The man, his best friend, her brother, waved at him, then placed his arm around her shoulders and guided her into the fire station.

This woman had known more pain than she ever should have and it was his fault, his responsibility, his burden for the rest of his life. The rapist was in jail for the rest of his life, and Chase was in a prison without bars for the remainder of his years.

CHAPTER ELEVEN

DAYS LATER, Chase warmed up in the racquetball court at the community center. He wasn't the kind of man to join a gym, no matter how convenient it seemed to be. With his schedule it wasn't worth it, and he liked supporting his local community. So he utilized the center whenever he could, like today.

Whap. He hit the ball again with a satisfying slam. This was the way men worked out their issues, by beating something up, even if it was something as insignificant as a hard rubber ball in an enclosed court.

The door opened, and Danny entered. "Starting without me?"

This was their usual date and time. Sometimes they jogged, sometimes they played racquetball, depending on their moods and the weather. Today it was pouring outside, the gloom moving in from the ocean like a living creature sweeping over the land. It matched his temperament.

"Yeah. Feeling stiff, so thought I'd warm up." Partially true.

"You know, stretching helps." *Whap.* Danny entered into the game when the ball came in his direction.

"So I hear." The words Emily had said echoed in his mind. *You'll be a stiff old man unable to tie his own shoelaces.*

"Uh, so how's it going with you and Emily?" Danny whacked the ball.

"What do you mean?" Had she spoken to Danny about them?

"At work. How's work going?"

"She's a great nurse. New skills these days."

"The martial arts?"

"Yeah. She's a regular ol' ninja nurse." *Whack.* "Impressive."

"She is. For more than just that."

"You never did answer my question about why you didn't tell me she was coming back."

"Figured you'd find out soon enough. You hadn't asked about her for a while. Figured you'd moved on, and I didn't want to get in the middle of it."

Moved on. How do you move on from the love of your life?

"I thought I had." The thought cramped his gut. He'd tried. He'd tried entirely too hard, especially in the beginning, but now seeing Emily again made him want to take it all back and try harder, try to be the man she'd needed him to be back then and he hadn't been. But it was too late. She'd made that clear the other day.

"And now?"

"Don't know."

They finished their game sweaty and worn out, then dropped onto a bench and cooled off.

"Think I'm gonna hit the shower here. Amber doesn't like it when I come to her place after my workout. Says I smell like a goat," Danny said with a grin, and took a sniff at one of his armpits. "She's probably right." He cleared his throat. "So, uh, you didn't really answer my question, either."

"Which one?" He knew, but stalled.

"About you and Emily. What's going on?" Danny didn't look directly at Chase, but bounced the ball between his feet.

"Don't know. Spent some time with her at the studio the other day. She taught me a few moves."

That got a reaction out of him and a rise of his brows. "That's amazing. I thought she'd karate chop you to pieces."

"She probably should have." That made him smile. The thought of her as a trained martial artist was fascinating.

"So what do you think? Going to get back together?"

"No. I don't think so. After that she withdrew, wouldn't talk to me, and I haven't seen her since." The real question was did he want to? They were vastly different people now.

"She's changed, that's for sure. But she had to. You know that, right?"

"I know. It's almost painful to watch her now, though." He rubbed his face with a towel. "Like she's still struggling every minute with the past riding on her back."

"I think she is. The physical stuff healed, but it's the stuff on the inside that's still broken." Danny sighed, leaned forward and placed his elbows on his knees. "It's been a long couple of years for her, but sometimes when I look at her I wish the old Emily was still there, still in there."

"After something like this I don't know if she can be *that* Emily ever again. She's tried to tell me that, and I'm not sure I was listening." He'd thought about it. She'd alluded to it. He just had to accept it or move on. Again.

"The new Emily is pretty awesome, though. Tough as nails. She even took me at arm wrestling."

"Yeah. She is." Flashes of her in the ER, in the apartment, and in the shower hit him hard. "Well, I gotta roll." He stood. He didn't have anything else he needed to do but he couldn't sit there anymore, ruminating about the past and his poor performance, his contribution to Emily's attack, and his unforgivable absence during her recovery. That was what killed him most. He hadn't been there for her.

He shoved out the doors of the community center into the drizzle, which had turned into a downright downpour. He made it to his car and got in, turned on the engine and let the wipers do their work. The heat of his body and the rain misted up the windows. He reached out to wipe some of it away with his hand and froze.

It had been a day exactly like today, three years ago, that Emily had been attacked. His heart thundered in his ears as he listened to the blast from the defroster trying to keep up with the condensation on the windshield. Frozen in the driver's seat, he sat there as memories of the past washed over him. Guilt he'd thought had been long ago dealt with ripped through him with the precision of a surgical blade.

It had eviscerated him then and nearly gutted him now.

He'd raced off in the early morning hours to the hospital, just as always, and had forgotten to lock the door of Emily's apartment, his mind occupied on the day ahead. Her place had been closer to the hospital and when he'd been on call he'd sometimes stayed with her.

He'd run into surgery and saved the day the way he was supposed to. As soon as the case had finished he'd been called to the ER for another emergency, but had been cornered by the attending physician before he'd been able to see the patient.

Unprepared for what he'd been told, he'd nearly dropped to his knees in disbelief. He'd raced to the side of a woman lying on a gurney in the ER, bloodied, battered, on the ventilator and disfigured beyond recognition.

"That's not Emily," he'd said, and had stormed out. "How could you misidentify a patient like that?" The force of his anger had sliced through him at such an egregious error, but the look on the face of the man he'd known and trusted had made him stop. The trembling inside him had escalated, and he'd looked back at her. "Is it?"

The remembered fear, the remembered pain of seeing her like that made him clench the steering-wheel now. How could he have not recognized the woman he loved?

But he'd expected to see her the way he'd last seen her, beautiful and lively. But she'd been near death from the injuries sustained in the attack in her own home.

Both of her eyes had been swollen shut, bruises had covered her face, and blood had trickled from her mouth around the breathing tube. The ambulance crew had placed a neck collar on her for transport and it had been stained red. Her nose had been swollen, obviously broken, and her lips had been cracked and bleeding in several places.

Dumbfounded, he'd moved forward in a fog and picked up one of her battered hands, seeing the broken fingernails, the abrasions and cuts. The ring he'd given her the previous Christmas had screamed out to him from beneath dried blood. "Em?" His voice had cracked, then he'd whipped around to the physician. "Is she going to live?"

"We don't know." It had been the bald truth.

Those words had just about killed him. She'd had to go to surgery to repair a broken jaw, multiple lacerations in her mouth, a broken nose and plastic surgery for the lacerations on her face. Her parents had been hysterical when they'd arrived. Seeing their beautiful daughter mauled in such a way had been something no parent should witness.

The windshield began to clear, and Chase looked out at the day of drizzle and gloom, trying to pull himself out of the memory, but unable to as the rain drilled his car, drowning out all other sound. He covered his face with his hands, allowing the guilt of his responsibility to wash over him. Guilt, guilt, guilt. It hung on him like a worn and tattered coat he could never remove.

He should have taken the time to lock the damned door, but he hadn't. It *was* his fault.

Days had passed with Chase and Emily's families standing watch by her side until she'd roused from the coma she'd been put in by heavy sedation. The swelling around her eyes had improved, but they'd still been purple.

Over the next few months her physical condition had improved while the rapist had continued to terrorize his way through the city. He'd violated nine women before being caught for a traffic violation. Stupid, but par for the course.

Getting close to Emily after that had been hard. They'd tried to have a normal life again, but both of them had realized there was no normal any longer.

And he'd been an idiot. He'd been angry and impatient and unable to be the man, the friend, the support she'd needed at the time, and she had been right to kick him out of her life. The first and only time they'd tried to make love had been a disaster.

Her body had finally healed physically and they'd wanted to be close again, each of them aching for it, needing it, but not understanding how long it might take to get there. She'd panicked. Even with the light on so she'd been able to see it had been Chase with her hadn't helped. She'd vomited when he'd touched her intimately.

All she'd felt had been pain and terror where once they'd experienced great joy together. All they'd had was great sorrow. The strangling sensation in her throat hadn't stopped and she'd screamed until she couldn't anymore.

He'd left then, left because he'd been afraid. Afraid of the demons inside her that might never go away. And he'd been selfish. Wanting her back to the same old Emily had been ridiculous. He'd had no concept of grief or recovery of this magnitude. Grief worked in strange ways and now, looking back, he could see it had been his grief that had overwhelmed him and made him act in ways that hadn't served him or Emily.

Weeks had passed, and she hadn't contacted him. He hadn't called her, wanting to give her some space, and then he'd heard she'd taken off on a travel assignment. Without saying goodbye. He'd been hurt beyond measure, but had covered it up with more anger and by convincing himself it had been her loss.

That was when he'd started on a womanizing spree, trying to bury himself in any woman so long as she hadn't reminded him of Emily.

Chase sighed, turned down the defroster and put the car in gear. Once out of the parking lot he didn't know where he was going, where to go, but found himself driving past Emily's apartment, and discovered her car wasn't there. Minutes later he found it at the martial-arts studio where his car had mysteriously driven to. Puzzled at his need to see her again, he entered and sat on a bench outside the workout room.

Inside the glass-walled studio he found Emily. She hadn't seen him, didn't know he was there, and he could watch her without disturbing her.

"Today is a women-only day. No men allowed." Rose approached and sat on the bench beside him.

"What?"

"It's Wednesday. Women-Only Wednesdays. No testosterone allowed in the studio." Though she gave him the info, she didn't look like she was going to toss him out on his ear.

"I'm sorry. I didn't know."

"She's very strong, you know."

Chase turned back to watch Emily as she led a group of women through poses and exercises. "She is. More than she ever was."

"That's because she's done the work." Rose peered at him, looking like a bird contemplating a bug it was about to eat.

"Training, you mean? I can see that."

"She's done the physical training, yes, but she's done the emotional and spiritual part of it, as well. Still continues to do it daily."

"Therapy, you mean?" He'd suspected that.

"Yes, and meditation, and giving over to the universe that which no longer serves her. The anger and the fear. 'Whoever can see through all fear will always be safe.' That's a quote from *Tao Te Ching*, by Lao Tzu, a very ancient, very wise man."

"I never thought of it that way."

"No. You would not have because you have not done the work she has."

"Excuse me?" Really? Had she just had the gall to say that to him? After all he'd been through, after all he'd lost?

"It's true, but you don't want to admit that, do you? You have not done the work she has, so she is further ahead in her recovery than you are in yours." Rose shrugged as if it were a simple thing.

"I see." Anger began to fill him.

"No, you don't see, which is why you need to come back on Manly Monday, a men-only day, and begin your own recovery."

"I don't have the time for that sort of thing." Frowning, he turned away from Rose. Some *sensei* she was.

"Then you will never recover, and you will remain stuck where you are in this life." She stood. "Until you deal with an issue, it will continue to show up in your life over and over again. Then you will be forced to deal with it at some point and it will be more painful for you than if you had dealt with it when you were supposed to."

"You're a pretty smart woman, too." He nodded, acknowledging some part of what she said rang true for him, and the anger fizzled away. Dammit. He hated being wrong and he hated being told he was wrong even more.

"Because I, too, have done the work."

Recovery. He'd not thought of it that way, that he needed to recover from the trauma that had affected Emily, from the powerlessness of it, the helpless way it made him feel. Squirming a little on the bench from the discomfort of his thoughts, he stood, not wanting to violate the Wednesday rule.

The restlessness that had been invading him all morning eased. Now that he'd seen Emily, seen her in her element, he could go on with his day in peace.

With his heart somehow lighter, he walked out into the rain.

Chase got to work early the next morning, anticipating seeing Emily. The anticipation humming through him was a new yet familiar sensation but one he hadn't experienced in some time. He felt happy, and for the moment peaceful.

Patients seemed to whiz by him all day long until he felt a change in the atmosphere of the ER. It became heavy, serious, quiet. Uncomfortable.

"What's going on?" he asked Liz. As the charge nurse, she knew everything going on.

"Rape victim came in from the university. Apparently, she went to an event last night on campus, but when she woke up this morning she had empty spots in her memory. She feels like she engaged in sex, but has no memory of it, and may have been raped."

"Oh, jeez." Inside, Chase's guts churned. "Do we have any female docs on right now? Who's going to do the rape kit?"

"No, I was going to see if you could help out. Emily's in there with her now, doing the preliminaries."

"*Emily?* That's not right. Isn't there a way to find a woman to help out? I can do it, but she will probably be very uncomfortable with it." This was not a road he wanted to go down unless absolutely necessary. Perhaps this was what Rose had talked about yesterday.

Emily approached them, her face stoic, and she was a little pale. "I agree. There's a SANE hotline number we can call and find someone to come in and perform the exam."

"Sane? What's that?" Chase asked.

"Sexual Assault Nurse Examiner. I've taken my training, but haven't tested yet, so I can't officially do the exam, and not as a travel nurse. My company won't let me." She shifted her position from one foot to the other. "I can call the center. They always have someone on call who can come do the kit and collect evidence."

Chase nodded, and so did Liz. "Go ahead. Give them a call."

"We get this kind of patient so infrequently I don't know if we have an official policy about it."

"It happens more than you know, so there should be a policy and one nurse on every shift who is the designated nurse for rape victims." Emily offered the advice and it was good.

"There's no nice way to put that, is there?" Liz asked.

"No. Sexual assault and rape are not nice things to put a nice label on, anyway," Emily said, her face becoming pink and her eyes glittering with anger. "People need to be held accountable for their actions. Too often things like this are brushed aside as boys being boys, when it's really an act of violence."

"If this upsets you, Liz will assign you to another patient," Chase said, and kept his voice calm and clinical.

"It's not the patient that upsets me. It's the lack of knowledge and the act itself that anger me." She held onto the counter and took a few deep breaths. "I'm sorry. I shouldn't let my personal feelings affect my work."

"It's a terrible thing for her," Liz said. "Do you know if they will also do counseling? Can you set that up for her, as well?"

"Yes, the SANE nurse will do preliminary assessment and then get her set up for further support."

"Boy, you know all kinds of stuff!" Liz said. "Good thing she ended up being your patient, or we might not have gotten her the right attention."

"I'm glad I'm with her, too."

"Let me make that call so I learn the process." Liz stepped around the desk, and Emily faced Chase. The compassion in his eyes was almost her undoing, almost led to her falling apart when she couldn't afford to and almost made her want to reach out to him.

"Are you okay? This can't be easy." The energy coming off him was pulsating, almost as if it put its arms out to surround her with an energetic layer of protection.

"I'm okay." She nodded and took a deep breath. "I'm okay, but later I might need some down time."

"If you need to meditate, I'll watch her for you."

"Thank you." That spontaneous offer created a warm pulse in her chest and made her heart beat a little faster.

"I know it hasn't been easy on you these last few years, but you've come an amazingly long way." His gaze dropped from hers for a second and then he looked at her, fierce and intent. "I want you to know I'm so proud of your accomplishments."

Her jaw dropped for a second, and her eyes went wide. "What?"

"I want you to know I'm…proud of you, Em. You're doing so much to help other women, and you're so much stronger than you ever were." His voice cracked with emotion and tears sprang to her eyes unexpectedly.

"Thank you, Chase," she whispered, and took a step back from him. She needed the distance, the distraction, the space between them or she was going to come unglued. "Please let me know when the SANE nurse is here. I'll be sitting with the patient until then."

Turning, she hurried away from him and the emotions swirling around him or she was going to get sucked back into the vortex of the past.

By the end of the shift Emily felt like someone had beaten her with a hammer. Every possible body part hurt, even her hair felt like it was on fire. The energy of holding back her emotions, keeping her past memories at bay was exhausting work. She gathered her belongings and headed out the door.

"Can I talk to you?" Chase asked, hurrying to catch up to her in the parking lot.

"Did I forget something?" As tired as she was, it wouldn't have surprised her.

"No, I just wanted to see you before you left."

"About what?" Puzzled, she stopped in the light of a streetlamp. From habit, she always was aware of her sur-

roundings, never putting herself in a potentially dangerous situation by standing in the shadow.

He fidgeted, ran his hand through his hair the way he
did when something bothered him. "That patient today,
the...the..."

"The rape victim? You can say the word to me, Chase.
It's just a word."

"Okay, then, yes, the rape victim. I didn't know how
sensitive you were going to be about that, and I didn't want
to say anything if it was going to bother you."

"Bother me? What bothers me is people walking on
eggshells around me, thinking I'm so fragile that one word
will break me." She turned and kept walking to her car.
"That's what bothers me."

Chase followed along. "I don't know what to say to you
sometimes. All I can think of is, 'Will this bother you?' or
'Will that bother you?' I'm trying to be considerate about
this, but I don't know what to do."

"I'm not fragile, and you just need to be yourself around
me." She paused and pushed her hair behind her ear. "I
mean, if you want to be around me."

Without speaking, he closed the gap between them and
put his arms around her shoulders, drawing her closer,
slowly but firmly until their energies mingled and his
chest pressed against hers. "I do, Em. I do want to be
around you. So much it hurts."

With her defenses so low, that was all it took to break
her. She huffed out a breath and took in another one and
another that were sharp and short, and tears filled her eyes,
her chest burned, and she cried out when she wrapped her
arms around his middle. "Oh!"

They stood that way, holding each other in the parking
lot, while Emily cried. He felt the tremors in her body as
her tears saturated his shirt, and he soothed her by strok-

ing her shoulders and the back of her head, keeping his hands to the upper part of her body and offering her comfort the only way he knew how.

"I hate this, you know?" She pulled back, sniffing.

"What?" His voice was a whisper, and he tipped her face up to his.

"Crying. Serves no purpose. I'd rather hit something."

"It's a release, and one you apparently needed." He pulled out his shirt to examine the wet splotches on the left shoulder area. "I'm happy to be your handkerchief."

"Oh, stop," she said, and frowned, then a laugh bubbled up inside her. "Just stop."

"Or, what, you'll laugh? How tragic is that?" Smiling, he gave her another nudge.

"Chase!" The giggles seemed to have a life of their own and took over her body as she wiped the heels of her hands against her eyes, smearing her mascara down her face. "Oh, my God, I can't stop." She turned away from him and kept moving to her car, but it didn't help. The laughter followed her.

The man kept following her and the grin on his face was something she thought she'd never be happy to see again, but she was and it was beautiful.

"Don't stop, Emily, don't ever stop."

"Stop…what?" She pressed a knuckle to her mouth and bit on it, hoping to stop the cascade of giggles with pain, but it wasn't working.

"Don't ever stop laughing, finding joy in the little things, the stupid things in life. They matter."

And that was what stopped her laughter. "I did. For a long time, I did." Taking another shaky breath, she began to get control of herself again.

"I know, and I'm sorry. I'm so sorry I wasn't there for you when you needed me to—"

"You okay, miss?" A security guard pulled up in a white van.

"Uh, yeah, I'm okay," Emily said, and took a step back from Chase. And then another.

"Okay. Parking areas can be dangerous, so I'd like to see you safely in your vehicle."

"Thanks, anyway. I think I've got it from here." She waved him away.

"If you say so," he said, and pulled away to patrol elsewhere.

"Emily, will you go out with me?" Chase asked, and his brows rose, like he hadn't meant to ask that question.

"Will I go out with you?" Was he *serious*?

"Yes."

"Like on a date?"

"Yes, like on a date." The smile that moved his mouth sideways had always been a heart-killer for her and it was no less forceful on her now. "Friday. I'm in surgery all day tomorrow, but Friday would work."

"That's like in two days." An eager trembling began in her stomach. Anticipation filled her even though she hadn't said yes yet.

"It is. I'll pick you up at five, we'll go have dinner in Virginia Beach, then take a walk by the ocean, watch the sunset."

"Chase…" she began, not sure how to handle this situation. She didn't want to hurt him, but she didn't want to hurt herself, either, then she remembered a previous engagement. "Actually, I have an event Friday night. There's a fundraiser for the rape crisis center. I go every year."

"I see." A mask covered his face. "I could go with you."

"I already have a date." *Squeal.* She did, but it wasn't what he thought it was.

"I see," he said again, looking closed and distant.

She couldn't mislead him on purpose. "Okay, so Danny is my date, all right? Maybe another time. Like Saturday night?"

"I will hold you to that," he said, and the expression on his face changed, his eyes glittering with something she couldn't identify. It wasn't sneaky or sinister, but there was definitely something going on in that brilliant mind of his.

"Okay. Okay." She quickly unlocked her car, got in and locked it again. She had to get away from him before she did something stupid. Something out of character. Something wild and wanton. Her body began to hum as she drove home, still charged from the contact she'd had with his body. Although it had just been a hug, it hadn't been just a hug, and they both knew it.

It had been the beginning of something she wasn't sure she wanted, but wasn't sure she didn't want either. The next time they were together could be combustible, and she had to prepare herself for it before it swept her away.

CHAPTER TWELVE

FRIDAY ARRIVED AND Emily spent half the day congratulating herself on maintaining her dignity and the other half berating herself for not inviting Chase back to her place for the night. What had been there between them in the past had been good. Not perfect, they'd had their issues, but they'd liked and respected each other, and *that* had been the basis for their relationship.

She went to the studio to work out the angst and sexual hunger that had kept her awake for half the night. That worked, then she'd showered, eaten a light snack and now waited for Danny to pick her up in his hopefully clean car. Their parents would meet them at the hotel ballroom. They had been pillars of support for her in her recovery and had been staunch volunteers at the rape crisis center ever since. Although they'd never been involved in an organization like that, there was only one way they could see to give back to the people who had saved their daughter's life. With their time.

With a last look in the mirror, she declared herself fit to go to a black-tie event. Her hair had been spiked to perfection and sprayed a bit, the tips blonde, the base auburn, and it suited her but made her look a bit like a pixie. The makeup she had applied was subdued with just a dash of sparkle at the corners of her eyes and cheekbones.

The only really good piece of jewelry she'd indulged in was a large black pearl she'd found at an estate sale and it hung now on a delicate silver chain around her neck. The pearl itself lay perfectly between her breasts, which looked more voluptuous than they really were thanks to a lacy push-up bra. Once in a while she indulged in the feminine and enjoyed it thoroughly, when it was safe for her to do so. When she could just be herself, she enjoyed herself more.

The dress had been a find at a vintage store. It had been an indulgence, but she didn't care. She felt beautiful in it and that was enough reason to wear it. The black lace bustier hugged her torso and cupped her breasts as if it had been made for her. The skirt fell in flirtatious waves of satin past her knees to a respectable tea-length, mid-calf. When she spun around the dress moved with her, the skirt flaring out and making her feel like she'd been thrown back in time to when dancing had been an art form.

Danny knew she loved to dance and would be her partner until the band quit playing or they dropped dead from exhaustion.

Little black bag. *Check.*

Lipstick. *Check.*

Little black shawl. *Check.*

Keys, a little cash and her ID. *Check, check, check.*

She was ready, just waiting for Danny. When the doorbell rang promptly at six, she was surprised. For him to be ten minutes late was not usual. For him to be exactly on time was a miracle.

She grabbed the doorknob and opened the door. "You're really on time…"

Chase stood in her doorway.

In a *tux* and her jaw dropped.

She'd never seen him look more handsome. Ever. Ever. *Ever.*

"Good evening, Emily." Even his voice sounded husky and sexier than she'd ever known it.

The hair on her arms and the back of her neck stood straight up, a flash of desire shot straight to her groin and her mouth went dry. "What are you doing here?"

"We should get going, or we'll be late. Traffic can be a bear when there's a football game at the university, and we have to pass by there to get to the hotel."

"You didn't answer my question." That was true, but she still proceeded as if she were going somewhere with him.

"I know." He stepped forward and escorted her out the door, then took her keys, locked the door and placed the keys into her purse. "I'll tell you on the way."

Dumbfounded, Emily allowed him to lead her down the stairs to the parking lot and to a very shiny black limo. *Squee!* The driver stood beside the back door and held it open, an enigmatic smile on his face. "Evening, miss."

"Good evening." The only proper way she knew to get into a vehicle in formal attire was to sit, then swing her legs inside, *à la* Marilyn Monroe, Hollywood style. A ridiculous giggle erupted in her throat. She felt like a movie star!

Chase entered right behind her and settled so he could look at her.

"You look stunning, Emily. Absolutely stunning." His gaze traveled over her body, and he gave an appreciative whistle.

"Yes, well, thank you." Nervous when the car moved forward, she tried to tuck her hair behind her ear, but it wasn't long enough to tuck. "You don't look half-bad yourself." Indeed, the black tux against the crisp white shirt was just devastating to her senses, as was the cologne he wore. It was her favorite, and he knew it. He'd always worn it when he'd wanted to tempt and tease her, torment her senses. It worked now as well. She was definitely tempted.

"So, are you going to tell me what's going on?" Soft, soothing music began to play in the vehicle. Chase handed her a champagne glass and reached for the bottle she hadn't seen until now.

"Yes. Your brother couldn't make it, so he asked me if I would give you a ride."

"Some ride." Her eyes widened as suspicion mounted.

"Isn't it, though?" He poured champagne halfway up the glass, then poured some in another for himself. He clinked her glass with his. "Cheers."

"What happened? He arranged to have tonight off weeks ago." She'd nagged him until he had, too, or he'd have forgotten.

"Apparently, one of the guys was hurt, and he's covering an extra couple of shifts to help out. This happened to be one of them. Unfortunate, don't you think?" Chase raised his glass and drank, but kept his sparkling gaze on her.

"Terribly. Lucky for me you could fall on your sword and sacrifice yourself for the good of others, right?" Emily drank from the glass and let the tiny bubbles work their magic on her anxiety at seeing Chase in such a surprising manner. Her heart fluttered wildly in her chest and a flush seemed to overcome her body. Maybe it was the effects of the champagne, though she'd only had a sip, or maybe it was Chase, but either way it was exhilarating. Living in the moment had its benefits.

"Exactly. I do love to support my community when I can."

The driver negotiated his way around the stadium traffic and delivered them to the front doors of the Williamsburg Governor's Mansion, the fantastically elegant historic structure very close to the historic section of town that had been built over two hundred years ago. The evening had begun to chill, but with the fizz of the champagne and her dashing companion she really didn't notice it.

"Allow me." He held out an arm to escort her formally into the ballroom, where he handed over their tickets to the person at the front. She was a woman, mid-sixties, with sparkling blue eyes and a winning smile.

"Welcome! Have a wonderful evening, and thank you so much for supporting our event."

"What a nice woman."

"Her daughter was raped and murdered."

Chase did a double-take. "Are you sure? She looks so happy."

"Oh, she is, because of the assistance of the center. She's one of the board members and is a driving force to keep the place going."

"Looks can sure be deceiving."

"You aren't kidding. She put her anger to good use."

"Maybe we should send her to congress. She'd get some things accomplished."

She stopped, her face serious. "Chase, stop a minute."

"What?" Puzzled, he raised his brows at her. Nothing had changed, but she was dead serious.

"I just wanted to thank you for coming. You didn't have to, but it means a lot to me that you're here."

Touched at her words, he cupped his hand against her cheek, allowing himself the softest touch. "There's no place I'd rather be."

Before Emily could response to the kink in her stomach they were overcome by a group of attendees in high spirits. Mostly ladies, but a few men rounded out the group, who were laughing and hugging and carrying on with each other as if they were old friends. Soon they were swept away by the tide of people and conversation became impossible as the volume in the ballroom grew to disturbing proportions.

Chase disappeared for a few moments but returned with two glasses of champagne and handed her one. "Trying to get me intoxicated, are you, Dr. Montgomery?" For some reason the vision of him handing her a fluted glass evoked the playful side of her that had been buried for some time.

"Just wanting you to relax and enjoy the night."

"Indeed."

"Are you?"

"I am." She accepted the glass from him and a thrill of sexual energy shot through her as his fingers lingered on hers. It was just a touch, just a whisper of his skin against hers, but it was enough to make her take a step closer to him. The energy humming off him came in waves of heat that literally made her want to be closer to him, to reach out and trace the lines on his face that hadn't been there three years ago, to push away the fatigue etched in his brow and trace her thumb over those lips of his.

Swallowing took great difficulty as Chase held her gaze. He didn't move, he didn't speak, nothing in him changed, yet everything in her did in that moment.

"Isn't the champagne to your liking?" With one finger he reached out and touched the bottom of the glass, raised it toward her lips. She parted them and let him tip the champagne into her mouth. She swallowed without taking her gaze from him. "It's perfect. Everything is just perfect."

Intense, Chase held her gaze and the energy between them nearly crackled. He leaned forward, but didn't touch her. His cologne swirled in her mind, evoking feelings from the past she'd thought had been cremated and set free in the wind.

"So are you."

Unable to think of anything clever to say, she guzzled the rest of the champagne and then took a few breaths. "Wow." The buzz in her head was nothing compared to the buzz in her groin.

"Hey, here they are!"

She turned at the sound of her brother's voice. Astonished, she suddenly wished for more champagne and clutched Chase's arm as he drew near. She waggled her glass at him. "I think I'm going to need more of this."

Approaching them were her brother in a tux, a sight she'd never seen before, his girlfriend, looking stunning in a red sheath, and, gulp, her *parents*. The hostility between her parents and Chase had been overpowering in the early days of her recovery. They had held him responsible for the attack, and she'd been caught in the middle of it.

Now, who knew what was going to happen? They'd realized it hadn't been his fault, but by then she and Chase had split up. She stiffened as they approached. Danny grabbed her into a big brotherly hug.

"What's going on?" She hugged him, then pulled away and slugged him in the shoulder the same way she had when they had been kids. "I thought you had to work, big fat liar."

"I was, but there were too many guys covering shifts, so I volunteered to take off." He held his arm out to his girlfriend. "You remember Amber. Let me introduce you to Emily's date, Dr. Chase Montgomery." Danny introduced them, and Chase shook her hand, said a few polite words, but remained in close proximity to Emily.

Then Chase did something that surprised her and made her very proud of him. He strode toward Emily's mother and father, held his head high and his shoulders firm. "Mr. and Mrs. Hoover, it's nice to see you again."

"Why, Chase! I didn't expect to see you here tonight." Her mother gave the exclamation, her eyes soft and her smile pleasant. Then she did something that shocked Emily. She hugged Chase and patted his back. An act of forgiveness and acceptance. The work of the center was clear in that gesture.

A waiter going by with a tray of champagne slowed down long enough for Emily to grab two more glasses of it. She was going to need them.

And then her father, the tough nut that he was, reached out to shake hands with Chase. Two of the men she'd loved most in this world faced each other as true gentlemen. Tears clouded her eyes, and her heart pounded mercilessly in her chest. If she hadn't had two hands full of champagne, she'd do something, at least wipe away the dribbles of tears running down her face and ruining her makeup.

Forced to abandon one of the glasses, she set it down on the table closest to her and dabbed at her eyes with one of the linen napkins. She swallowed and took a few deep breaths. She had to control herself, control her emotions, control all those feelings bubbling to the surface that she totally hadn't expected and totally wasn't prepared for.

"Hey, you okay?" Amber asked, and patted her shoulder.

"Yes, yes, thank you." She pulled away from Amber and blew her nose on the napkin. "I don't know what happened."

"Chase happened. That's what," Danny said, and took the second glass of champagne and gave it to Amber. "Caught you off guard, didn't it?"

"You could say that." She controlled herself and watched as Chase approached. "You could definitely say that."

CHAPTER THIRTEEN

CHASE WORE AN enigmatic expression as he left her parents. She opened her mouth to say something. She didn't know what it was going to be, but she was interrupted by someone speaking from the front of the room. "Attention, everyone, please take your seats. We've a lovely dinner for you, so please enjoy."

The usual mayhem ensued where people found seats and conversations changed topics while the servers set plates in front of everyone. The clatter of utensils on plates was a low undertone as people ate more and talked less.

"It's so nice to see our young folks together and dressed so nicely, isn't it, Bob?" her mother Lois observed. Though her mother had been a homemaker and had never experienced trauma the way Emily had, she had stood firm with her daughter through the entire court process and had been more of a rock than Emily had ever known her to be.

"It is. And looking pretty snazzy, too, I might add," her father said. "Haven't seen either of you dress up like this since your proms."

"Don't remind me," Danny said. "That tux was horrible."

"Have any pictures?" Amber asked, and waggled her eyebrows at Danny. "I'd love to see them some time."

"I kept some, just in case I needed to blackmail him later in life," Emily said. "I can email them to you, Amber." She winked.

"You. Did. Not." Danny stared at her, mouth open and eyes wide in shocked horror.

"What are big sisters for, anyway?" She laughed and it felt good to share this night with this company in this way.

After dinner the speakers began by thanking the patrons and attendees, as well as the volunteers and the other people who made the whole place run efficiently. While the band got organized, people shuffled together and broke into small groups.

"Anyone else need more champagne?" Chase made the offer and only Emily nodded. "I'll be right back."

Chase stood in line at the bar, listening to the conversations near him. He had to take a deep breath as he overheard a woman talking about the reason she was there.

"Yeah, I thought he was a good guy. Seemed nice enough, but when I said no, he went off on me."

"I'm just so glad you were able to find help at the center."

"I would have killed myself if I hadn't found them. I was on the verge of it when I had my first meeting." She gave a caustic laugh. "Going to the center was actually a last-ditch effort before doing something terrible to myself."

"I'm so glad." The women hugged.

"So am I. My life is different now for sure, but so much better than I could have ever imagined. I'm even going to take a self-defense class too. Can't wait."

Chase closed his eyes, not wanting to hear the pain of the women expressed so openly, but it was unavoidable as he stood in line right beside them. And it was more humbling than he could ever have imagined. He'd been such an ass back then. Such a complete and utter ass. No wonder Emily had left him in the dust. He'd deserved it.

"What can I get for you?" the bartender asked. "More champagne?"

"Yes. Two, please," Chase said absently, as conversations around him buzzed in his ears.

"Excuse me," a man said. He was tall, carried himself well and looked vaguely familiar. "Aren't you Dr. Montgomery?"

"Yes," Chase said, nodding, wondering if he'd taken care of the man as a patient in the ER at some point.

"I'm Mark Hampton, Detective Mark Hampton. I worked your girlfriend's case. Emily Hoover, right?"

"Yes. That's her." Words had difficulty forming in his throat as Chase was instantly transported back to that time and the guilt that washed over him. Guilt that had never resolved.

"She's one remarkably lucky woman."

"Really?" Chase couldn't fathom that.

"Really." Mark moved closer and the two men stepped aside where they could talk without being overheard. "She was the first victim. As bad as her injuries were, she survived by her wits and her personal strength. The longer he went without getting caught, the more violent he became. You may or may not know, but he killed the last two." Mark's face was stern, his eyes cold as he talked of the man who had nearly ruined Emily's life.

"I didn't…I didn't know." That took a minute to sink in. Oh, God. If it hadn't been for his one careless mistake that day, things would have been completely different.

Mark huffed out a long sigh. "Take good care of that woman. She's a fighter. That's what got her through the whole thing." He shook hands with Chase and walked away.

All of the people in this room had in some way been

affected by a sexual assault and the traumatic aftermath. It was staggering, looking around at the number of people who were here, who were victims, friends or family of victims and had come in support of something that needed to be brought from the shadows into the light.

"Here you go."

Chase paid the man and took the drinks back to Emily. She simply shone like a light tonight. Though dressed all in black, it suited her and was a striking contrast to the vibrant color of her hair, her eyes, the ruby lips. The strength of heart and soul shone in her tonight. He was dumbstruck by her.

She was anything but a victim, and he was so proud of the accomplishments she'd made it nearly staggered him. As he approached, she looked up. The expression on her face froze, then molded into something else, something he hadn't seen on her face in some time.

Female. Gloriously female. Confident in her body, her mind and her heart, she stood there, silently declaring she was whole once again.

"Thank you," she said, and accepted the glass, just as the music started.

Danny grabbed the glass from her hand and set it down before she could take a sip. "Come on, big sister. This one is mine." He dragged her out onto the dance floor before anyone else got there and spun her around several times.

Chase watched as she grinned and the two of them fell into a routine they'd obviously done many times in the past to a song about shaking it up. Chase shook his head. Things were definitely shaking up in his life since Emily had returned and he didn't think he ever wanted to go back to the way it had been before.

Three songs into it, Chase had had enough and cut in

on Danny. "You have your own girl to dance with. She's looking awfully lonely over there by herself."

"Oh, good point. Better go take care of my lady and you can take care of yours." With a gallant bow, Danny placed Emily's hand in Chase's. "Now, get to it."

Gladly, Chase eased into position with his right arm around Emily's waist and her right hand cupped in his left.

"You're gorgeous, and I've been a complete idiot."

"I like the first part, but not the second." She placed her left arm on his right shoulder and moved with him to the music. There was a light sheen of perspiration on her brow and the lighting picked up some sort of sparkle at the corners of her eyes. The pixie was emerging.

"It's true." They moved on the dance floor together, remembering how to move as one, and in seconds their bodies melded together in time with the music as if they'd never been apart. "I have to admit it, admit my part in our breakup."

"It's blaming, Chase. In the therapy I've taken, blaming doesn't work for healing. Forgiveness does."

"Don't tell me you've forgiven that bastard." Righteous indignation burned white hot in him.

"No. I will never forgive him for what he did to me… to us, and my family. Never. I'm still working on letting it go." She took a deep breath and pressed her right temple to his right cheek. "But I've forgiven *us* back then. The people we were couldn't cope with what happened, and I've let it go." She cupped his cheek. "I want you to let it go, too. For you and for me. It wasn't your fault, ever."

He pulled back slightly to look at her face. Nothing except serenity showed, and he returned to his position with her cheek against his, her arm around his shoulders and his hand splayed on the small of her back.

"Let go, Chase."

"I don't want to let you go." Not yet. Not when he had her in his arms. He couldn't.

"I mean the pain. It's the only way you'll heal. The memories will always be there, but will fade away if you lay down new memories on top of them. Kind of like paving a new road in your mind."

"I...I haven't done that." Thoughts of other women in his life the past few years were meager at best. Memories had power and emotion associated with them, and he hadn't built any new ones. Hadn't wanted to, had simply roiled in his pain.

"You need to."

"I will. Starting now." He closed his eyes, savoring the sensations of her in his arms, the way her body felt and moved in time with his. Right now. This was a memory he wanted to keep in his brain forever.

The night progressed, and they danced, drank champagne and danced some more. Tonight Emily felt freer than she had in the past three years. She laughed, her spirit was light, and she needed nothing else, aside from being in Chase's arms on the dance floor.

Her parents said their goodbyes after a few dances, but Danny and Amber still hung in there on the dance floor. As the night wore on, the tempo of each song seemed to get slower and more intimate. More attendees left, dwindling down to just a few couples hardy enough to stick it out until the very end.

Reluctant to leave just yet, Emily wanted to have just a little longer in Chase's arms. She didn't know where things were heading with him, if anywhere, but right now, living in the moment, in *this* moment, it was pure bliss.

"Hey, I think they're gonna kick us out now." Danny approached them with Amber clinging to his side, looking lush and in love. "We're gonna head out."

"Okay. Good night." Emily extracted herself from Chase's embrace to hug each of them. "Be safe."

She turned back to face Chase and had to catch her breath. The way he looked at her right then she almost felt like she was being devoured. "Guess we should call it a night, too."

"I'll call the limo and have it meet us out front." He led her to their table and collected her wrap, placed it around her shoulders, then frowned. "Hmm. That's too bad."

"What?" She looked down at the black velveteen shawl. "Did something get spilled on it?" She couldn't see anything.

"No." He gave a wistful sigh and brought his gaze to hers. "It just covers up too much of your skin."

"Oh." She held his gaze. "You liked that, did you?" Flirty and playful weren't her norm anymore, but tonight, right now, it was perfect.

"Very much." Casually, he appeared to be tying a knot in the middle of the wrap, but he traced a finger over the curve of her right breast and down into the dip of her cleavage, then up over the curve of her left breast.

Tingles flashed through her nipples and shot straight to her groin. Savoring the sensations, she leaned closer to him, wanting more, aching for his touch against her skin again. "Perhaps we should go."

"That's a fine plan." Casually, he placed one hand on her back and escorted her to the door. Once seated in the limo, her heart raced, her mouth went dry, and she pressed her lips together, eyes on Chase, who leaned against the seat in the corner. He took her hand in his and tugged a little, urged her closer until she leaned forward and placed her weight on her hands on the seat.

Teasing him was fun and made her feel sexier than she'd ever felt before, especially in recent memory. "What can I do for you, Dr. Montgomery?" She licked her lips and watched his gaze linger on them.

"Nothing. Absolutely, nothing." He untied the knot of the shawl at the front of her chest slowly, allowing his knuckles to rub against her dress. With talented fingers he eased the knot free and let it drift away, exposing her décolletage to his gaze. Turning his hands, he used his thumbs to stroke the rising curves of her breasts, pushed up by her bra and enhanced by her position.

She closed her eyes, allowing the sensations to flow over her, to bubble up within her, and became familiar with them again, as they had been strikingly absent for too long. When Chase bent his thumbs and used them to draw down the edge of the dress and the bra, he teased her nipples at the same time. Leaning forward, he stroked his tongue around her nipple on one side, then licked his way over the curve of silk lace to her left breast, stroking his tongue across the other nipple.

"Oh…oh, my." Trembling on her arms, she wasn't prepared for the onslaught of emotion and desire he unleashed in her with that simple action.

"Don't move."

"I don't think I can." He pulled down the front of her dress on the left and took her entire nipple into his mouth, teasing, stroking, suckling it, and desire shot white-hot through her body straight to the core of her. With her hands still holding her weight, she really couldn't move as he eased that side of her dress up and revealed the other side to his gaze and his mouth.

The hum of the car engine changed and the vehicle slowed. Chase eased her dress up and retied the knot of her shawl in the front.

"We're here." She sat up straight and gathered her purse in front of her, certain she looked like she'd been fornicating in the back of the car—which, really, she had been. "Will you come in for a while?"

"I'll take care of the driver, then I'll take care of you." He leaned forward and pressed a firm kiss to her lips, then pulled back.

They emerged from the car into the cool night air, which felt pleasant against her skin and a refreshing boost to her brain. He took her hand and tucked it into the crook of his arm as they approached her apartment.

Her hands fumbled with the keys and he took them from her, unlocked the door and escorted her inside. "Don't be afraid of me, Em. Ever."

She barked out a nervous laugh. "It's not you I'm afraid of."

"Then what?"

"Me."

CHAPTER FOURTEEN

CHASE LEANED BACK against the door. "You're going to have to explain that one. Communication needs to be very clear between us. I don't want anything to go wrong between us now, not when we're starting to find each other again."

Before answering, she put her purse and shawl on the counter and eased her feet out of the killer pumps, letting her feet return to their natural shape. Chase watched, his eyes glittering as she removed each piece of clothing.

"That's better." She wiggled her feet in the carpeting.

"Don't stop on my account."

She tossed a look his direction. "Nice try."

"So why don't you tell me what you mean?" He removed his jacket, hung it on the door behind him. He moved into the living room, pushed the coffee table away from the couch and settled onto the floor. He was relaxed and confident and reminded her of the other day when she'd taught him some relaxation techniques.

Hesitating, Emily followed him. She removed her watch and placed it on the coffee table, followed by her earrings and pearl necklace.

Although he looked calm, she was a mass of churning nerves inside. This man had been her lover, and her friend, and right now she wanted to reach out to him more than ever, but she held back, with three years of pressure churning inside her.

He'd also burned her more than anyone ever had. Though she'd forgiven him, taking that first step was a doozy. Trust was a huge deal. One minute she wanted him, the next second fear overwhelmed her.

"I don't think this is a good idea after all. Why don't I change my clothes, and I'll take you home, or you can call a cab. That would be best." Decision made. She headed to her bedroom, but Chase quickly caught up to her.

"Don't do that to me, Em. Don't do it again."

"Do what?" She backed up against the doorframe to support herself.

"Shut me out like that. Like you're doing right now."

He was angry. More angry than she'd ever seen him, and her instincts kicked in. She took a protective stance. "Back off."

"Emily…" He reached for her again.

"I said back off, Chase." She raised her arms and parted her feet.

"I said you shouldn't be afraid of me, and I meant it. I'm not going to hurt you." He took a step away from her, respecting her boundaries, but inside he shook, the power of the emotions coursing through him making him tremble. He clenched his hands into fists at his sides and wanted to punch something.

He flashed around and faced her. "Hit me."

"What?" Confusion covered her face, and she backed up a step, but still kept her stance. "No. I'm not going to hit you."

"I said hit me." He moved closer and closer until she was cornered.

"I'm not going to—"

"It's the only way you're getting out of this tonight.

You're going to have to hit me." It would feel better if she did. It would be some relief if she would. "I'll feel better if you do."

"Chase, no!"

"Emily!" He grabbed her hand and placed it against his chest. "Please…" His voice cracked. "Hit me. I need you to."

"No, that's not why I'm here, not why I came back here. I didn't come to punish you."

"Then why did you come back here, Emily? Why?" Frustration oozed from every pore. He had to hear her say it.

"This is my home, too, you know." She relaxed a little, but her eyes were still wary and bruised with remembered pain and she curled one hand into a fist.

"There are several hospitals where you could have worked, yet you chose the one I'm at." She tried to move around him, but he countered her move.

"I wanted to be where I was comfortable, where I knew people." She tried to go around him again, but he blocked her movement. "I was tired of learning a new hospital with every assignment, so this was easier."

"Liar. After the last hurricane and reconstruction, it's totally new."

"But I didn't know that." Or had Danny already told her that, and she'd forgotten?

"Liar."

She jumped like he'd shocked her and stomped her foot. "I am *not* lying."

"Yes, you are. You came to where I was because you wanted to see one thing. *Me*." With that, he reached for her and dragged her against him, catching her off guard before she could react. "Tell me I'm wrong, Emily. Tell me you don't want me anymore and I'll go and never bother you again." His voice broke and his heart raced. His breathing was harsh in his chest, but so was hers. "Tell me you don't still love me," he whispered.

She clenched her teeth and tears filled her eyes as she stared at him. "I. Can't." Her breathing was ragged, making her breasts rise and fall enticingly.

"Then let me love you, Em, let me love you." He cleared his throat when his voice cracked again.

She licked her lips, and her gaze dropped to his mouth. "I just wish…" A caustic laugh escaped her throat, and she relaxed, leaning further against him, letting her body get to know his again. "I wish…"

"I know, baby, I know." His gaze dropped to her mouth, that luscious mouth he'd used to love exploring his body. With one hand, he cupped the left side of her face and neck. She pressed her face against his palm, closed her eyes, and his heart broke. "Emily." Bridging the slight gap between them, he drew her face forward, hesitated. "I really want to kiss you."

"Kiss me." The words were a breath that released him.

The first touch of his lips against hers felt somehow foreign, as if he'd never been there before. He hadn't, not in this way. The last time he'd kissed her she'd held back. Now he moved in, relaxed, opened himself up to her as he never had.

Soft and sweet, her lips parted, and he met her tongue with his, eased against hers, glided together, stirring his passion for her that he'd thought had died and now surged strongly within him. A moan stirred in her throat, and she pulled back from him, blue eyes startled and fiery.

"Oh, God, Chase, what have you done?" Her thumb stroked his lower lip.

"What do you mean?" His breath was tight in his throat, his heart catapulting in his chest and his body aroused beyond belief. Had he somehow misunderstood the words *kiss me*?

"You've freed me." This time she wrapped her arms around his shoulders and hauled him to her, her mouth searching for his.

Eagerly, he met her, one hand against the small of her back, the other cupping the back of her head. This was no small kiss but a barn-burner, setting them both ablaze. Passion unleashed between them had always been stimulating, but now there was a fire between them that wasn't going to be easily contained.

He backed her against the wall, needing the stability before his legs gave way. She was so sweet, so special, so beautiful.

Mouths searching, hearts aching, they found a way to the path of forgiveness they'd never imagined. Once the light had been shined onto the trail to lead the way, there was no turning back.

She pulled away and held him close. "Oh, God, Chase. I'm so scared, but so turned on, I don't know what to do."

"Why are you scared?" That puzzled him.

"I haven't been with anyone since our last time, since before…" She met his gaze full on. "You're the last man I made love with, and I don't know what to do, how to do it anymore."

That stopped him a second. Compassion for her swelled within him. She wanted him, there was no doubt, but this moment was precious, and he didn't want to mess it up.

"Let's just go slow, and you be the guide."

She kissed him again then, soft, slow. Each touch, each sigh drew them closer together.

He struggled to keep his hands on her tiny waist, until she reached for one of his hands and guided it upward to cover her breast. Allowing her head to fall back, she took in a breath and let it out slowly. The angle of her head, of her neck, the light perspiration on her skin made him want to take a bite out of her.

Her nipple stirred beneath his thumb. He could feel the lace of her bra through the dress and his curiosity was roused beyond belief. Using the tip of his thumb, he hooked the front of her dress and drew it down, exposing the lace of a dangerously red bra. The cup seemed to only be half-there, pushing her breast upward, firm and ripe, toward him and his mouth actually watered.

"You're beautiful, Em."

She was ready, she wanted him, and he leaned down to satisfy himself. To take her nipple, barely hidden by the very edge of the lace, into his mouth.

The feel of Chase's tongue on her breast nearly made her climax at once. He teased a lazy path over the crest of her right breast, his tongue dipping beneath at last to tease and stimulate her nipple. Then with a very clever use of his thumb he tugged the cup downward slightly and sucked her nipple into his hot mouth.

She actually jumped, as if the last bits of her soul had suddenly returned to her body. The feelings were so intense, so pure, so passionate. She'd never expected to feel this way again, this excited, turned on and wanting. Her body hadn't forgotten after all. Her body had waited for the right man to bring it to life again.

The dress was of no further use to her and it needed to go. Fortunately, the material had an abundance of stretch and forgiveness in it. Reaching up with her left hand, she clasped the neck and dragged it down, shrugged, and the garment lay in a heap at her feet.

"That's certainly convenient."

"Indeed." She almost didn't recognize her own voice, so deep and husky, filled with desire.

Chase, being a man to take advantage of opportunity, used the thumb of his right hand to trace the edge of the left cup of her bra, teasing that nipple, as well.

He didn't kiss her again, but watched her, and she kept her gaze on his face. "You're beautiful. You're luscious. And I want to make love with you."

Nodding was about all she could do, and she licked her lips as his head dipped downward again to her left nipple this time. Slowly, languidly, he traced and teased both of her nipples until she was certain they would never go down again.

This time, when he pulled back, he looked down over her body, over her abdomen that quivered slightly with her breathing, the curve of her hips, and lingered on the red thong she wore.

"I'm surprised. A thong?"

"Hate panty lines."

"Me, too." His gaze wandered further down her thighs and calves, all the way to her red toenails. "I like this look, a lot. You're strong and capable and independent, beautiful and passionate."

Trembling, she reached out to his clothing to find his skin beneath the tux shirt. She wanted to see him, all of him, and wanted him against her. Soon his shirt was gone and the button on his pants hung open. There was little between them now and this was her opportunity to stop.

"Are you okay?" With one finger, he blazed a trail between her breasts and headed south, downward over her abdomen and belly button, then paused at the edge of her thong.

"I'm good." She licked her lips. "Very good." She closed her eyes and felt him move.

He was on his knees in front of her and his mouth hit her abdomen, where he rubbed his face against her skin, placed searing kisses there, tugging with his teeth at the ring in her belly button.

His hands came up the backs of her thighs to cup her buttocks. With his breath hot on her skin and his fingers doing their best to drive her crazy, Emily nearly fainted with wanting him.

Each touch brought them closer, each kiss made her want more. Slowly, he clasped the waistband of the thong in his hands and eased it down until it joined her dress on the floor at her feet.

"Turn into me," he whispered against her skin. She knew what he wanted, and she wanted it, too. Turning her hips forward, she waited until his breath was hot against her skin and heading downward, over her mound. Trembling, her thighs parted, unable to contain herself. "That's it. Easy, babe. Just let go, just enjoy. Let me please you."

With one hand he cupped her bottom and pulled it forward, with the other hand he parted her feminine flesh and pressed his face toward her. The first touch of his tongue seared her and she sucked in a breath through clenched teeth. "Oh, God."

"Nice, huh?"

"Yes. Oh. Oh. Yes." She sank her hands into his hair, needing something to hold onto as she let go and let him have her body. For the first time she could let go.

Legs unable to hold her weight up any longer, she began to slide, easing her way down the wall. Going with her, he adjusted his position and somehow they made it to the couch nearby. Down on his knees in front of her, he scooted her hips to the edge of the cushion and resumed his quest.

"Relax. Enjoy." He kissed his way up her right thigh to the juncture, then returned to her left knee, repeating the same trail there, upward. She needed this so badly, and she needed him more than she wanted to admit. And then he was opening his mouth over her center again, hot and wet, tongue searching for her bud, circling it, teasing it and driving her wild.

The pressure, the electricity built within her, and when he eased a finger inside her sheath she gasped and nearly screamed with the power of her climax, the first one she'd had since back then. Passion overwhelmed her, and she cried out. Pulses of white light and pure energy formed in her core and pulsed outward. Chase held on to her as the orgasm released inside her.

Then he moved upward toward her. "Are you okay?"

"Yes. Very." She moved to lie back, and he stripped and adjusted position and placed his body over hers, moving until his erection lay against her thigh. Swollen and needy, he wanted her, but he didn't, couldn't, rush her.

"Come closer." He adjusted his position. "Closer." Again he moved upward until the tip of him brushed against her at her apex.

"I want you inside me, Chase. Now." She felt like she was losing her virginity all over again. Somehow he managed to dig a condom out of his pocket and put it on. She was glad he'd thought of it as she hadn't, hadn't even considered she was going to be making love tonight. Feeling Chase ease slowly inside her, carefully, made her want to cry. For the things they had lost, for the pain they'd experienced and the chasm that had developed between them.

"Keep your eyes on me. Focus on me, on us. I want to see you."

She did. The connection with him, the fullness he created inside her, the stretch of her body to accommodate him kept her focused on him and only him. On the sensations pulsing between them, drawing open that door that had been closed between them.

Something in his eyes changed as he eased fully inside her.

Sweat popped out on her skin at the weight of him and a choking sensation closed her throat. The room spun around her, and she couldn't breathe. Eyes wide, breath strangling in her throat, panic threatened her mind and she turned her face away and scrunched her eyes closed as images of her attacker flooded her mind.

"No. No!" Frantic, she pushed at his shoulders, tried to get him off her.

"Stay with me, love. Emily, stay with me."

"It's…your weight." Being pressed down into the couch was what had done it, reminding her of the assault, taking her back to that awful night. Struggling to push it away, she battled to rise. "Get up, get up!"

He backed off and sat, his hands raised, waiting for her to make the next move. She straddled his thighs, taking control of the situation, her position facing him.

"Better?" His voice was soft, a mere whisper in her ears, encouraging her to proceed.

Chase kept his hands on her hips and pulled a nipple into his mouth again. "Oh, that's it, that's what I want, what I need."

Slowly, she rose up onto her knees and his erection sprang upward between them. She positioned herself to allow him to enter her, and she angled her hips back and forth, teasing him, teasing herself with him, becoming more comfortable with the feel of him inside her as she eased onto him.

He threw his head back against the couch, drawing his breath in through gritted teeth at the exquisite torture.

His fingers dug into her hips with the effort to control his body, control his mind.

When she was ready, when the moment was right, she took him fully into her and waited until her body molded around him. "Oh, my, Chase."

"Emily." He pulled her forward to kiss her, to plunder her mouth with his, and she gave him back everything she had. Hips angled, he pulled her back and forth over him, stimulating her flesh, and she clutched his arms.

"Oh-God-oh-God-oh-God." She was going to climax again and she let her body go as she never had before. Chase clutched her hips and kept the pace up until she was nearly exhausted, and the trigger of her climax clicked. Pulses of heat, electricity and pure pleasure swept through her as she came. Her sheath clutched him over and over again until he stiffened and cried out with his pleasure.

Pulsing and electric, he released, letting her body work him over until he was just a mass of twitching nerve endings.

Hot and sweating, they clutched each other. Chase moved his arms upward to clasp her around the middle and began to rock her. Rocked back and forth, pushed her hair away from her face and pressed a kiss to her hand.

And she cried. For the first time since the rape she cried in his arms. His heart broke and tears filled his own eyes at the anguish and sorrow unleashed. The sound of her sobs would never leave his mind or his heart, and he knew he was responsible for them. Back then she'd wanted to forgive him, but he hadn't been able to let her. Now he didn't know. The pain was still so sharp.

"I'm so sorry, Emily. So, so sorry."

Some moments passed as he held her, rocked, listening to her tears and releasing his own that had been pent up.

"This was beautiful, Chase, and something I didn't know I needed. Thank you."

Pushing her damp hair back from her face, he used his thumbs and wiped away the tears making black trails down her face. "Seriously?"

"I never thought I'd make love again. I'd convinced myself I didn't need sex, or the physical contact with a man anymore, that I'd had enough in the years we were together."

"That's just sad." He raised his brows at her, trying to make her laugh. There was healing in laughter as well as tears.

"I know, right?" She laughed, then tried to take a breath but snorted instead. And that made her laugh again, and Chase watched the joy of her unleash in his arms.

He laughed too, like he hadn't done in years.

CHAPTER FIFTEEN

THEY STAYED UP for half the night, showered together, made breakfast and coffee at 3:00 a.m. and then finally slept, cuddled together naked.

Emily slept like the dead for the first time in three years. No dreams, no nightmares, no waking up trembling from some unfamiliar noise she'd heard in the dark.

Chase slept deeply contented, with no haunting feelings of loss, of pain, or emptiness surrounding his mind or heart.

They woke to bright sunshine streaming in the window. Gone was the gloom of the past few days, and the overcast atmosphere had given way to the bliss of an Indian summer. The morning was half-gone by the time they roused, and dressed with a side trip to Chase's townhouse for a change of clothing and his running shoes.

What was supposed to have been a leisurely walk around the park ended up as a competitive sprint, with Emily in the lead and Chase bringing up the rear, snagging her around the waist and dragging her to the grassy lawn. "Caught you!"

With a squeal she tumbled to the ground with him, gasping for breath.

People raced and ambled around them. On a Saturday there were all kinds of people out there in the park with them. Moms with babes in strollers, young people chasing Frisbees and throwing balls for dogs to retrieve.

The sound of thundering footsteps neared them as two young men chased around. One held up a beanie high in the air, like he was running across the finish line of a race. "I got it now, sucka!" Laughter followed him, and so did his companion.

"Come back here, you. Bitch!" The second young man raced after the friend with the hat. "You bitch, I'm going to get you!"

The smile on Emily's face froze and her eyes widened, her breathing came in short little gasps. A humming began in her ears and drowned out everything else. She rose from the grass and began walking. She didn't know where, didn't know why, but she had to move, had to leave, had to get out of there. The sensation of panic, choking, drowning saturated her and stole the breath from her lungs.

Someone grabbed her by the arm and stopped her. Panic and finely tuned instincts surged to the surface. She lashed out with her fists and knocked Chase on his ass. "I told you not to touch me!" She stood there, hands in fists, legs braced apart as if she were going into battle.

"Emily. Wait. It's me. It's Chase." He jumped to his feet, rubbing the center of his chest where she'd hit him.

"What?" The haze of panic began to lift, primal, protective instincts began to recede, and the world came back into focus. *"What?"* She blinked several times, looking at Chase as if she didn't know where she was.

"Focus on me." He panted, but kept a short distance from her.

"Why are you looking at me that way?" She took in a deep breath and blew it out, tried to get her heart to stop racing and quieten the buzz in her ears.

"Are you okay now?" Concern emanated from his face.

She looked around at the blue sky, the changing leaves on the trees swaying in a light breeze, the people moving around them. "I don't know what happened." She took a step closer to him and raised a hand to her forehead. "Chase?" Starting in her middle, the tremors began.

"Can I touch you now? Are you okay with that?" He held his arms out and let her move into his embrace when she was ready to.

Hesitating, deeply saddened, and shaking, she allowed her body to touch his and slowly raised her arms around his middle, and pressed her face against his chest. The thumping of his heart was strong in her ear, and she closed her eyes as he put his arms around her.

"What happened?"

"I...don't know."

"We were having a good time, then those two guys with the beanie ran by, and then you panicked." He rubbed her back.

It all came back to her in an instant, and she pulled away from Chase. "We need to go now. I need to go home now. Or take me to the studio." With quick strides, she began to walk away from him, but he kept up with her.

"Okay. I'll take you home. I'll take you to the studio, whatever you need—just tell me what happened." They arrived at the car and he unlocked it and opened her door, but she didn't get in.

The space was too confined, too narrow, too dark, even on such a bright day. "Maybe I'll just walk home."

"Nonsense. If you aren't ready to get into the car we'll wait. It's okay."

Anger flashed inside her like a lightning storm over the Chesapeake Bay. "It's *not* okay. It'll *never* be okay." She slammed the door shut and covered her face with her hands. Tears hit like a storm, and she screamed until she thought she couldn't scream anymore. Down on her knees, she couldn't press back the force of the emotions swirling like a deadly tornado inside her.

"Emily, Emily!" Chase knelt near her and called her name. "Emily. Honey. Stop crying. Please, stop crying."

Finally, his voice and his words penetrated her mind. *Breathe, just breathe.* The voice of her *sensei* entered her mind, emerged from the depths of the place she'd crawled into when she'd first entered her recovery. She took a breath, then another and another. Controlling the shaking in her limbs was quite another issue. "Okay. Okay." Tears still streamed down her face, but her breathing was better.

"That's it." His voice was soft and soothing to her, the same way Rose's had been, and she turned into him now, pressed her face into his shoulder and allowed him to help her up. "Can you stand?"

"Yes. I think so." She nodded and clutched his arm. Then he placed his other hand at her waist and helped her back to the car. He opened the door, but before helping her inside he opened both windows all the way.

"This might help." He assisted her into the passenger seat, reached in to buckle her, then hurried around to the other side of the vehicle, got in and pulled out of the parking lot. "Where do you want to go?"

"Take me home."

"Okay. Do you want to go to the studio?"

She took in a few breaths. "No." Her voice was flat and unemotional, reminding him of times past. "It's too crowded there today. Too many people. Just take me home."

Minutes later he unlocked the door to her apartment, pushed it wide, and they entered. "You can go now." Emily started for her bedroom.

"No. You stay put. I'm going to check out your apart-ment, make sure everything's okay. Then we'll talk."

Emily ignored him, her brain paralyzed by the event at the park. She needed her control, needed her armor on to protect her. Now. Shucking her clothing, she put on her *gi* and tightened the belt around her waist.

For the first time in an hour she could take a deep breath, felt the energy of who she was now flowing over her as if it poured over the top of her head, down her shoulders and all the way to her feet, encapsulating her in the protective shield she required for her personal safety. She'd momentarily forgotten it.

With her eyes closed, she stood by the bed and focused, turned inward. Raising her hands against her shoulders, palms facing out, she slowly moved her hands away from her body as if she were pushing out of a balloon, enlarg-ing her energy to a larger bubble. Another deep breath, and she could feel the presence of her new self returning to her, having been temporarily displaced.

"How are you?" Chase spoke from the doorway.

She opened her eyes, blinked, having forgotten he was there. Then it all came back to her and her shield pulsed strongly, more protectively around her. "You can go."

"I'm not leaving you." He took a hesitant step forward. "What happened back there? One minute we were having a great time, and the next you weren't there."

"It doesn't matter." She brushed past him to the living room and spread out her meditation mat, sat down on the edge of it. Her feet were tucked beneath her, and she sat back on her heels, something Chase was certain would cause him considerable pain, but she moved into the po-sition as if she'd been doing it for years. Maybe she had. Hell, there was so much about her he didn't know right now, but really, really wanted to. If she would let him.

He sat down on the other end of her mat with his feet extended.

"I said you can leave now." The only things that moved were her mouth and her eyelids opening. "I actually *need* you to leave." The tone of her voice was flat, unemotional, controlled.

"I'm not leaving." He kept his tone even, his eyes on hers, but inside he raged, at the universe, at the rapist, and the society that had made such a creature, but mostly at himself for not seeing her PTSD when he'd needed to. It all made sense.

"I left you before, and I'm not doing it again."

"You think you're helping me right now, but you're not."

"I don't know that I'm helping you, but I want to. Something set you off back there, and you need to talk about it. I'm here, and I don't have to be anywhere until Monday morning." He spread his hands out in front of him. "Tell me."

"No."

"Emily, holding stuff like this inside you only gives it more power."

"Like you'd know anything about it." Anger finally blazed in her face, seeming to shoot out the ends of her hair, the blond tips looked like they were on fire.

"Why don't you tell me?" Now he kept his voice modulated and calm, not reacting to the emotion in hers. He needed to be a rock for her now.

She closed her eyes, shutting him out. Okay. If she wouldn't talk, he would. "I wanted to kill him. I wished I had found him and killed him myself."

She took a deep breath and let it out slowly.

"No, you wouldn't have. It's not you, not who you are."

"I wanted to."

"So did I. For a while, then I had to let it go so it didn't rule my life." She opened her eyes, now calmer, and he could almost see the energy swirling around her, soothing her, and he wished he could do that for her. The powerlessness he felt at the moment overwhelmed him, emasculated him and nearly drove him to his knees.

She was withdrawing into herself right in front of him, and he couldn't do a damned thing about it. She was back to the distant figure he'd known before.

"Come back, Emily. Stay here."

"I can't, Chase. Not right now."

"I'll wait for you here."

"No. You need to go. I'm fine." Another deep breath. She rose elegantly from her position. "If you care about me the way you say you do, you'll leave now and never come back. I don't want you. I don't need you." Tears filled her eyes. "I thought I could come back here and pick up with you, could have a relationship with you, but I realize now I can't. It's too much for me."

"Emily..." The pain in his chest was almost unbearable. He couldn't do it, couldn't walk away from her. "I do care about you, more than ever." How could he tell her he'd never healed, never recovered from the trauma that had ripped apart both of their lives?

"Then go." She took a breath, and he heard the jagged edges of it catch in her throat. "Please." Her voice was just a whisper, but it cut through him as surely as a scalpel would have.

Hurt, pained beyond comprehension, he went to the door and paused. "I'll leave, but not because I want to. We'll talk again soon."

"It's what I need right now." She stayed in the living room, keeping as much distance between them as possible.

He paused with his hand on the knob, took one long look at her, opened the door and stepped outside, then closed it behind him. He would wait until she locked the door before he left, he'd make sure she was safe this time.

Then something overcame him, in that nanosecond of waiting for her to lock the door, it possessed him at a cellular level and urged him to action. He twisted the knob and burst back through the door.

CHAPTER SIXTEEN

"I WAS ABOUT to lock that." She stood in the kitchen, her eyes wary, her body stiff and tense, watching and waiting for him to make a move.

"The hell you were. I'm not leaving. I love you, and I'm not going anywhere."

"Chase…" she said, and her voice cracked. "Don't say that. You don't mean it, and I don't want to hear it." Not now. Not ever. Never again would she set herself up for being hurt that way.

"I do, and I know you still love me. I don't know how I've gotten through these last few years without you." He gave a caustic laugh and looked down. "Actually, I do know. I was arrogant as hell. I don't know why you stayed with me as long as you did. I was an idiot for not being more patient, having more insight, and I don't know how you can ever forgive me."

She paused, her eyes narrowed at him, her face flushed. "Are you asking me *now* to forgive you when you wouldn't let me do it before?"

"No." Another harsh laugh erupted from his throat. "There's no way I'm asking that. No way you should do it. I'm just hoping we can move past this."

"Then what do you want? You wouldn't let me forgive you back then. If you won't now, there's nothing. Without forgiveness, there's no future for us, or anything." That was a lesson it had taken her a long time to understand. Letting go, forgiving. They were the same to her. But if he didn't allow her to forgive him and forgive himself, there was nothing for sure. Neither of them would have lives.

He raked both hands through his hair, then punched the air. "Hell, I don't know. I don't know, Emily, I just know I can't go on this way, pretending you don't mean anything to me because you do." He paced the kitchen several times, then clutched his hands to his head and yelled. "Argh!"

"Chase—"

"I can't take it anymore, Emily. I can't take it!"

"Then you have to let it go." Her voice was soft, certain and pure. He'd have felt better had she screamed and railed at him, validating his need to suffer.

"I can't. I don't know how." He paced again, wishing there was something he could do to get the demons out of his head and his heart.

Compassion overwhelmed her. This man had suffered nearly as much as she had, and she hadn't seen it. But there it was right in front of her, and she couldn't ignore it or him any longer.

"Tell me about it."

"I couldn't do anything. I couldn't help you. There was nothing. I couldn't operate on you, I couldn't put you back together. Other people had to do it for me. Other people helped you through rehab, your parents took care of your apartment. I was left out." He clutched the counter for support and dropped his head, panting as if he'd just run a marathon.

"I didn't need you to do anything, I needed you to listen and be present. Neither of us really knew how to do that then, but we're learning, Chase. We'll always have lessons to learn in life, and this is just one of them."

"I wanted to do something, and I couldn't." He took a breath. "That's not who I am, who I was."

"That's what I needed, who I needed you to be. Now I know you couldn't take on that role I was trying to force you into. I didn't know it, either."

"I *fix* things. I'm a surgeon. I cut things out or sew them up, make people better than they were before." He turned his head and pain-filled eyes looked at her. "I couldn't fix you."

"But I didn't need fixing, Chase. I needed to be listened to. I needed to be held, and loved, but mostly I just needed to *be*."

"You did, and it was because of me it all happened."

"Chase, it wasn't." Shock filled her at his admission. "You can't seriously believe that anymore."

"I'm the one who left the door unlocked. I was so focused on my work. The second I woke up I was gone mentally, I was out of there."

"That's not true." At least, not at the beginning of their relationship.

"It is! I have to admit it. Admit and accept my part in the terror that has become your life. I didn't listen to you, I didn't *hear* you. You would be talking to me, and I got so good at not listening I nodded in all the right places, and you never knew. When I got out of bed that morning it was no different. I was just gone, thinking of work, rounds, surgery, planning my day, and I left without making sure you were safe."

"Chase—"

"Don't! Don't say you forgive me because I can't bear the words." He hadn't forgiven himself. Would never forgive himself.

"It's not your fault. It was a simple oversight that you didn't lock the door. You were on an emergency call in the middle of the night, and there was a predator on the loose. You couldn't have known. No one did!"

"I should have protected you!" He grabbed her shoulders. "I should have kept him from hurting you, but I didn't, and I couldn't, and everything that's happened to you since that night has been my fault, my responsibility." He pounded his fist on his chest. "Mine."

"No, it wasn't then, and it isn't now. You couldn't have known. The serial rapist started with someone, and it happened to be me." She placed her hands on his arms, her touch gentle. There was no fear in her, no anger, just compassion for a man who was tortured by a burden that wasn't his to carry. The effects of the panic attack had worn off in her efforts to console Chase, and she was in control of herself again. "Look at me."

"No." He avoided making eye contact with her, but she put a hand beneath his chin and turned his face toward her.

"Chase, honey, please, *look* at me." Her voice dropped, emotion hung heavily in the air between them. "And *listen* to me."

After a few seconds he haltingly raised his eyes, damp with moisture, to hers. His breathing was harsh, his face was flushed, and he trembled.

"I'm listening."

"I forgive you, Chase. I forgave you a long time ago. When I tried to forgive you, you wouldn't let me and that's what drove us apart."

"Emily." He gripped her arms painfully, but she could take it.

"It was never your fault to begin with." Emotion tangled in her throat. "Never. I was angry at you at first. Really, *really* angry, but I came to understand it wasn't your fault or your responsibility. The blame lies in a man who is a predator."

Unable to handle the emotions churning in him, he clasped her against him, needing her strength, the amazing amount of strength she had to hold him upright. Tears leaked out of his eyes and the pressure of holding onto this responsibility for three years burst out of him in a powerful surge, leaving him breathless. He hadn't known he'd needed to hear her say those words.

His knees buckled and more of his weight went onto Emily, but she held on to him, she held him up and she used her strength to support him for a moment. Though she trembled, he could feel the strength in her muscles, and she stood firm. When his knees and legs were able to bear the burden of his weight again he pulled back from her.

Her face was a mess, and so was his. Hers had tears and red blotchy spots, and he was certain his face looked about the same. Pulling himself up to his full height, he cupped his hands around her face. "I'm sorry. I shouldn't have—"

"It's okay. I can take it. I'm stronger than I ever used to be, and for that I'm grateful. Very grateful." She smiled at him—it was soft and sad and bittersweet, but he could see the forgiveness in her eyes and knew it to be the truth.

"I am, too." He eased her closer. "I know I'm not supposed to touch you, but I have to do this." He pressed a very soft, very chaste, very heartfelt kiss to her forehead. For a moment neither of them moved, each caught in the power of that purity, that moment of grace between them.

When Chase pulled back, Emily wrapped her hands around his wrists and fresh tears fell from her eyes. "I am sorry. For everything." She took a breath. "This wasn't how our lives were supposed to have turned out. We were going to get married, have babies and live happily ever after, weren't we?"

"That was the plan." She moved away from him, needing a little space, a place to take a deep breath. "So what are you going to do now?"

"Go back to work on Monday, finish my assignment, maybe go on to another one after that." She shrugged. "I still haven't decided about where I want to put down roots again."

"This is your home, as you said, and you have as much of a right to settle here as anyone." He stepped forward. "Don't let that bastard run you away from your home again, Emily."

"I won't. I'm not." She cast a look over her shoulder at him. "Now I'm not sure working with you long term is a good idea, either."

"I see." He cleared his throat and took a step closer. "When we made love last night, it was beautiful."

"It was, and I thank you for that. For helping me get through that first time." She gave a small laugh. "Kinda felt like I was a virgin again."

"In some ways you were. You're a new you."

"True."

He clasped her hand and his fingers intertwined with hers. "Do you think…? Could you…?" He sighed. "I don't even know how to ask you this."

"What? It's usually better if you just ask things straight out."

"Emily Hoover, will you go out with me on a real date? Start over? Let me get to know the new you, get to know the new me?"

"I'm gonna have to think about that one." There was so much potential for pain.

"Really?" He pulled back, anger surfacing in his face. "I'm good enough to have sex with but you won't let me take you out?"

"That's not it. Not it at all."

"Then you'll have to explain it to me because I don't understand where you're coming from."

"I'm just trying to keep my life simple right now. Going out with you would complicate things. I know the other night I said I would go out with you, but now I'm not certain it's a good idea. For either of us."

"That's not a valid excuse." He stepped forward and cupped her face with his hand.

"I know, but I'm trying to come up with something." A sparkle returned to her eyes. Maybe there was hope for them after all. The power of the panic attack had been overwhelming and took time to recover from. Each time it would get better, but it would take time and patience.

"Then you'll go out with me? Let me try to make things up to you?"

"You can't make things up to me, because it's not your fault. Again. It's not your fault." She released his hand. "I don't want to go out with you if you can't accept that."

"It's hard." For both of them. They each had their own demons to slay, but maybe together they could do it.

"I know. It's very hard. I worked for a lot of months before I was even able to start to understand that." She blew out a breath. "I'm a whole person again. It's taken three years, but I'm whole. I'm not the woman I used to be. I'm different. I'm new. But I'm here. I want the same thing for you, too, Chase. But *you* have to want it."

"If you help me, I think I can do it. I can at least try."

"You thought you were my superhero, Chase, and you're not. You're just not."

"Well, thanks for *that* vote of confidence."

"Seriously. You're just a man, I'm just a woman, and that's all there is that needs to be there between us. You don't have to rescue me, and I don't have to be your salvation." She cupped his cheek and brought his face up to look at her. "We need to be who we are. Who we are *now*, not who other people *think* we are. And we can't be who we were back then."

"The question now is do you still love me? Can you love me again after all this?"

"We can't recapture what we used to have. We're different people now. You know that." As painful as that was, it had to be said out loud between them.

"Yes, but it doesn't answer my question." He faced her, cupped his hands around her face and drew her closer to him. "Look at me now and tell me you don't want me, don't need me, don't love me." It was a challenge for sure, but he needed it.

"I do love you, Chase." Tears rolled from her eyes down onto those beautiful cheeks, and he wiped them away with his thumbs. "I loved you then, and I love you now." She looked down then back up at him. "Thinking of you helped me get through the rough times. Thinking of the good times we had before it all came crashing down. In that way you were my strength."

"I should have been there for you." He gritted his teeth against the pain his actions had caused her.

"You couldn't. I was in survival mode. I couldn't take care of you and myself, so I took care of myself, and maybe I'm better for it."

"What do you mean?"

"I mean I needed more space than I knew at the time and if I'd been with you, maybe I wouldn't have found the strength to be who I am now, might not have found the courage to stand on my own, would have depended on you too much."

"We'll never know, will we?"

"No. And it's okay that we don't."

"We can't pick up where we left off, I know that." He

took a deep breath. "I'm seeing it. I'm okay with it." He didn't want her to leave again at the end of her assignment. "Will you stay awhile and let's see if we can really find our way back to each other again? I know you're only a few weeks into your assignment, but I don't want you to take off and go somewhere else when it's over. I don't know what the future holds, Em, but I want you in mine." He cleared his throat against the emotion trying to choke him. "If you'll have me. I want to be the man you need. Now."

With a gasp she threw herself at him. Trembling, they clung to each other as another layer of the past fell away from them. "Me, too. Me, too. But I think we should do some couples therapy at the center."

"Is that necessary, do you think?" He didn't know.

"I do. For you, for us together."

"Then we will."

"Thank you, Chase. It'll be good, you'll see."

"I do have one question." Chase said.

She snorted out a laugh. "Seriously? Just one?"

"Do you still have the ring I gave you?" He rubbed the ring finger on her right hand. "The last time I saw it was the night you were…you were attacked." Demons from that night tried to surface, and he let out a long breath. Somehow now they had less power than they'd used to, and he could push them aside for the moment. They might never go away and might try to take a bite out of him at times, but he had the strength now to vanquish them.

She rubbed her lips together as emotion overwhelmed her. "I have it. I didn't…I couldn't…get rid of it." Slowly, she pulled the chain she always wore around her neck and the pendant emerged from beneath her *gi*.

"Do you remember when I gave this to you?" He turned it over in his hand and examined the ring of promise he'd given her.

"I do. We were walking down by the river and it was the first time you said you loved me."

"May I?"

She nodded, and he reached behind her neck to open the clasp then slid the ring off the chain. "I couldn't wear it for a while so I put it on a chain, and then I didn't want to wear it, but I couldn't let it go."

He held out the silver ring with a single fire opal gemstone in the center. With his left hand, he took her right and slid the ring part way onto her finger. "When I gave you this ring, I gave you a promise."

"You promised your love, your faith, your fidelity and your honor." Tears that had been hiding beneath the surface surged over and trickled down her cheeks.

He huffed out a self-deprecating laugh. "I didn't do a very good job of keeping those promises." The trembling inside him bubbled up, but merged into a well of bounty and promise and hope for the future. It was still an unknown, the future, but with her by his side it no longer frightened him as much as it had.

He remembered the words from Lao Tzu that *sensei* Rose had spoken to him a few days ago, and though he hadn't understood them at the time they now began to make more sense. *Whoever can see through all fear will always be safe.* Now he could see the proof in Emily. She hadn't yet conquered all of her fear, but she had tackled the most dangerous of them all alone, and won.

"Circumstances weren't exactly conducive for either of us to keep any promises we made back then." She took in a shaking breath. The look in her eyes was soft and full of hope where just moments ago there had been none. Though he'd been partly responsible for it, he had to accept it was in the past and he couldn't change it, but he could change every day in the future by being present in it with her.

"I would like to make you a new promise, right now." The feelings in his heart swelled and his chest grew tight as the words emerged from someplace deep in his soul. There was no stopping them, and he'd never been more vulnerable than at this very moment.

"Chase, let's not make promises neither of us is prepared to make or keep. One thing I've had to learn is to live in the moment. Let's do that now."

"I'm prepared, and I will keep this promise." He cleared his throat and looked deeply into her eyes. "I promise to love you and respect you, to be your friend and your lover as long as you will have me in your life." He slid the ring the rest of the way onto her finger, then brought it up to his lips and kissed it.

"Chase Montgomery, you were the love of my life then and one I could never forget, no matter what happened to me or what happened to tear us apart." Tears lingered on the tips of her lashes, and she blinked to clear them away. "You hurt me more than anyone ever has, and you have the power to hurt me again."

Speechless, he opened his mouth to say something, but no words came out. Was she going to deny him now? Would she walk away from him again the way she had before? Anxiety stirred in his gut. *Please. Don't walk away from me again.*

"I can live my life alone, be without you, but I don't want to anymore." She placed her right hand on his chest and looked at the ring she hadn't worn in three years, then looked up at him. "I want you in my life, in my bed and in my heart."

"I don't know what the future will bring, but I want to be there for you, and you to be there for me." The anxiety lifted at her words, and he knew there would never be another moment like this one for them. Living in the moment. He had to learn to do that. With her new skills and her teacher's heart, maybe she could help him learn how.

She rose up on her toes and pressed her lips to his in a kiss of honor sealing their promise to each other. They didn't need a ceremony. They didn't need witnesses or a church for the vow they just made to be sacred. "I love you, Chase Montgomery, and I need you in my life."

"Emily." The joy that bubbled up in him was out of control. "I don't know what to say, how you can say that, but I'm so glad you did." He shook his head in disbelief. "I don't know where we're going from here, and I don't care. As long as you're with me I know we'll be okay." This was living in the moment, and now he knew what it was.

Unable to contain himself any longer, he kissed her deep and hard, wanting to impress himself on her and imprint her on him, wanting to fill his mind and his heart with all of her.

He wrapped his arms around her, and she clung to him. "I know we'll be all right."

* * * * *

MILLS & BOON®

Christmas Collection!

Unwind with a festive romance this Christmas with our breathtakingly passionate heroes. Order all books today and receive a free gift!

Order yours at
**www.millsandboon.co.uk
/christmas2015**

MILLS & BOON®

Buy A Regency Collection today and receive FOUR BOOKS FREE!

4 BOOKS FREE!

Transport yourself to the seductive world of Regency with this magnificent twelve-book collection. Indulge in scandal and gossip with these 2-in-1 romances from top Historical authors

Order your complete collection today at
www.millsandboon.co.uk/regencycollection

0915_ST19

MILLS & BOON®
The Italians Collection!

2 BOOKS FREE!

Irresistibly Hot Italians

You'll soon be dreaming of Italy with this scorching six-book collection. Each book is filled with three seductive stories full of sexy Italian men! Plus, if you order the collection today, you'll receive two books free!

This offer is just too good to miss!

Order your complete collection today at
www.millsandboon.co.uk/italians

5_ST17

MILLS & BOON®

Why shop at millsandboon.co.uk?

Each year, thousands of romance readers find their perfect read at millsandboon.co.uk. That's because we're passionate about bringing you the very best romantic fiction. Here are some of the advantages of shopping at www.millsandboon.co.uk:

* **Get new books first**—you'll be able to buy your favourite books one month before they hit the shops

* **Get exclusive discounts**—you'll also be able to buy our specially created monthly collections, with up to 50% off the RRP

* **Find your favourite authors**—latest news, interviews and new releases for all your favourite authors and series on our website, plus ideas for what to try next

* **Join in**—once you've bought your favourite books, don't forget to register with us to rate, review and join in the discussions

Visit **www.millsandboon.co.uk**
for all this and more today!

MILLS_WEB

MILLS & BOON®

MEDICAL ROMANCE™

THE ULTIMATE IN ROMANTIC MEDICAL DRAMA

A sneak peek at next month's titles...

In stores from 6th November 2015:

- **A Touch of Christmas Magic** – Scarlet Wilson *and* **Her Christmas Baby Bump** – Robin Gianna

- **Winter Wedding in Vegas** – Janice Lynn *and* **One Night Before Christmas** – Susan Carlisle

- **A December to Remember** – Sue MacKay

- **A Father This Christmas?** – Louisa Heaton

Available at WHSmith, Tesco, Asda, Eason, Amazon and Apple

Just can't wait?
Buy our books online a month before they hit the shops!
visit www.millsandboon.co.uk

These books are also available in eBook format!